The Lion
Book of World Stories

The Lion
Book of
World Stories

Retold by
Bob Hartman

Illustrations by Susie Poole

LION
Children's Books

For Princess Kari
and Prince Christopher

Text copyright © 1998 Bob Hartman
Illustrations copyright © 1998 Susie Poole
This edition copyright © 1998 Lion Publishing

This edition is published exclusively for the educational
market. This book is available in bookshops as *The Lion
Storyteller Bedtime Book*.

The moral rights of the author and illustrator
have been asserted

Published by
Lion Publishing plc
Sandy Lane West, Oxford, England
ISBN 0 7459 3950 3
www.lion-publishing.co.uk

First edition 1998
10 9 8 7 6 5 4 3 2 1

A catalogue record for this book is available
from the British Library

Printed and bound in Spain

Contents

Introduction   7

The Mouse and the Lion   8
A Story from Greece

Silly Jack   10
A Story from England

The Girl Who Played With the Stars   12
A Story from Scotland

Three Months' Night   16
A Story from North America

Arion and the Dolphin   18
A Story from Greece

Rabbit and Tiger Save the World   21
A Story from Puerto Rico

The Shepherd and the Clever
Princess   22
A Story from Finland

Tortoise Brings Food   25
A Story from Africa

Polly and the Frog   28
A Story from England

Rabbit and Tiger Go Fishing   31
A Story from Puerto Rico

The Mouse Deer's Wisdom   32
A Story from Java

The Four Friends   35
A Story from India

The Brave Bull Calf   38
A Story from England

Tiger Gets Stuck   42
A Story from Puerto Rico

The Clever Mouse   44
A Story from Wales

The Amazing Pine Cone   46
A Story from Finland

The Very Strong Sparrow   49
A Story from Africa

Simple John   52
A Story from Germany

The Selfish Sand Frog   55
A Story from Australia

The Mouse's Bride   57
A Story from India

The Big Wave   59
A Story from Japan

Tiger and the Storm   62
A Story from Puerto Rico

The Knee-High Man   64
A Story from North America

The Clever Baker   66
A Story from Scotland

How the Kangaroo Got Its Tail   69
A Story from Australia

The Greedy Farmer   71
A Story from Wales

The Generous Bird   74
A Story by Bob Hartman

Tiger Eats a Monkey   78
A Story from Puerto Rico

Lazy Tom   80
A Story from Ireland

The Contented Priest   83
A Story from Spain

Olle and the Troll   86
A Story from Norway

The Steel Man   90
A Story from North America

The Crafty Farmer   94
A Story from Japan

Tiger Tries to Cheat   96
A Story from Puerto Rico

The Two Brothers   98
A Story from Brazil

Kayoku and the Crane   101
A Story from Japan

The Two Sisters   104
A Story from France

The Selfish Beasts   106
A Story from Africa

The Determined Frog   108
A Story from Russia

The Robber and the Monk   110
A Story from Egypt

A Note from the Author   113

Introduction

In my work as a children's author and professional storyteller I have discovered that sharing stories with others is something very special. Stories can draw people close together, help them to share experiences and feelings, and take the imagination to far-away places and distant dreams. When my children were small, it was important to find just the right kind of story to read aloud. Sometimes that story climbed out of a book, and sometimes we just pieced it together ourselves—my daughter the princess and my son the prince, winging off on yet another adventure.

Wherever the stories came from, they usually had three traits in common—warmth, wit and wisdom. I think that stories need to have a good heart. They need to leave the listener with that safe, warm, happily-ever-after feeling. But that doesn't mean they have to be soft and sentimental—laughter is the perfect antidote for that. And if, in the midst of the laughter and adventure a child can discover something about bravery or honesty, kindness or forgiveness, hope or love, then there has been an opportunity not only to share a story and cement a relationship, but also to shape a life.

In my work as a storyteller I have gathered the stories in this collection from every part of the globe. Some of them may be familiar to you. But I hope that many more will be new—that you will share my delight in discovering them for the first time and also come to appreciate, as I did, how similar our dreams and values are, regardless of culture, nation or race.

So open the pages of this book and let's journey together to far-away places and once upon a times.

Because it's that special time—it's storytime.

Bob Hartman

The Mouse and the Lion

The mouse skittered left.

The mouse skittered right.

The mouse skittered round a rock and under a leaf and past the dark, wide mouth of a cave.

And then the little mouse stopped.

Something had grabbed his tail.

The mouse wrinkled his nose and twitched his whiskers and turned around. The something was a lion!

'You're not even a snack,' the lion yawned, as he picked up the mouse and dangled him over his mouth. 'But you'll be tasty, nonetheless.'

'I'm much more than a snack!' the little mouse squeaked. 'I'm brave and I'm clever and I'm stronger than you think. And I'm sure that if you let me go I will be useful to you one day. Much more useful than a bit of bone and fur that you will gobble up and then forget.'

The lion roared with laughter, and the little mouse was blown about by his hot breath.

'Useful? To me?' the lion chuckled. 'I doubt it. But you are brave, I'll give you that. And cheeky, to boot. So I'll let you go. But watch your tail. I may not be so generous again.'

The mouse skittered left.

The mouse skittered right.

The mouse skittered away as quickly as he could, and disappeared into the woods.

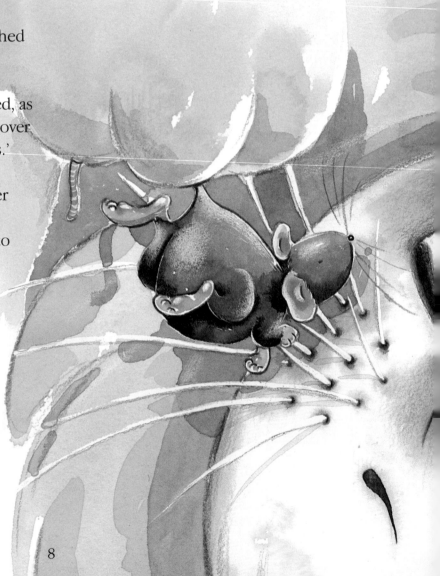

Hardly a week had passed when the lion wandered out of his cave in search of food.

The lion looked left.

The lion looked right.

But when the lion leaped forwards, he fell into a hunter's snare!

The ropes wrapped themselves around him. He was trapped.

Just then the little mouse came by.

'I told you I could be useful,' the little mouse squeaked. 'Now I shall prove it to you.'

The lion was in no mood for jokes. He could hear the hunter's footsteps. 'How?' he whispered. 'How can you help me, now?'

'Be still,' said the mouse. 'And let me do my work.'

The mouse began to gnaw. And to nibble. And to chew. And soon the ropes were weak enough for the lion to snap them with a shrug of his powerful shoulders.

So, just as the hunter appeared in the clearing, the lion leaped away into the forest, with his new friend clinging to his curly mane.

They returned to the cave as the sun fell behind the hills.

'Thank you, my friend,' said the lion to the mouse. 'You are indeed clever and brave, and you have been more useful than I could ever have imagined. From now on, you have nothing to fear from me.'

The little mouse smiled.

Then he skittered left.

And he skittered right.

And he skittered off into the night.

Silly Jack

On Monday morning, Jack's mother sent him off to work for the carpenter. Jack worked hard, and at the end of the day the carpenter gave him a shiny new penny.

Jack carried the penny home, tossing it in the air as he went. But as he crossed the little bridge over the narrow brook, he dropped the penny and lost it in the water below.

When he told her, Jack's mother shook her head. 'You silly boy,' she sighed, 'you should

have put the penny in your pocket. You must remember that tomorrow.'

On Tuesday morning, Jack's mother sent him off to work for the farmer. Jack worked very hard, and at the end of the day the farmer gave him a jug of milk.

Jack remembered his mother's words, and carefully slipped the jug of milk into his big coat pocket. But as he walked home, the milk splashed and splooshed and spilled out of the jug and all over Jack's fine coat.

When he told her, Jack's mother shook her head. 'You silly boy,' she sighed, 'you should have carried the jug on your head. You must remember that tomorrow.'

On Wednesday morning, Jack's mother sent him off to work for the baker. Jack worked very hard, and at the end of the day, the baker gave him a beautiful black cat.

Jack remembered his mother's words, and carefully sat the cat on his head. But on the way home, the cat was frightened, leaped from Jack's head into a nearby tree, and refused to come down.

When he told her, Jack's mother shook her head. 'You silly boy,' she sighed, 'you should have tied a string around the cat's collar and pulled it home behind you.

You must remember that tomorrow.'

On Thursday morning, Jack's mother sent him off to work for the butcher. Jack worked very hard, and at the end of the day, the butcher gave him a huge leg of lamb.

Jack remembered his mother's words, tied a string around the meat, and pulled it home behind him. But by the time he got home, the meat was covered with dirt, and good for nothing but to be thrown away.

When he told her, Jack's mother shook her head. 'You silly, silly boy,' she sighed. 'Don't you know you should have carried it home on your shoulder? Promise me you will remember that tomorrow.'

Jack promised, and on Friday morning, his mother sent him off to work for the man who ran the stables. Jack worked very hard, and at the end of the day, the man gave him a donkey!

Jack looked at the donkey. Jack remembered his promise. Then he swallowed hard, picked that donkey up, and hoisted it onto his shoulders!

On the way home, Jack passed by the house of a rich man—a rich man whose beautiful daughter had never laughed in all her life.

But when she saw poor, silly Jack giving that donkey a ride, she giggled, she chuckled, then she burst out laughing, right there and then.

The rich man was delighted, and gave Jack his daughter's hand in marriage, and a huge fortune besides.

When he told her, Jack's mother didn't shake her head. No, she hugged him and she kissed him and she shouted, 'Hooray!' And she never ever called him 'silly' again.

The Girl Who Played With the Stars

Once upon a time, there lived a little girl who wanted one thing and one thing only—to play with the stars in the sky!

Every night, before she fell asleep, she would stare out of her bedroom window at the stars dancing above her, and wish that someday she might dance with them.

One night, she decided to make her wish come true. So she crept from her bedroom, down the stairs, and out of the front door. And she set off to find her way to the stars.

The moon was full. The night was warm and bright. And it wasn't long before she spotted the stars— reflected in the water of a little pond.

'Excuse me,' she whispered to the pond, 'can you tell me how to get to the stars?'

'That's easy,' the pond rippled and shook, 'the stars come and shine in my eyes on most nights, so brightly in fact that I have trouble sleeping. If you want to find them, you're welcome to jump in.'

And so the little girl did. She swam and swam around that little pond, but she could not find a single star. So she climbed sadly out again, said goodbye to the pond, and set off, dripping, down the path.

Before long, she came to a little field. And there were the stars, dancing like tiny lights in the dewy grass. And dancing with them were the fairies—clapping their hands and beating their wings to the sound of harp and pipe and drum.

'Excuse me,' she called to the little people,

'I want more than anything to play with the stars. Do you mind if I join you?'

'Of course not,' the fairies called back. 'Come and dance with us as long as you like.'

And so the little girl danced. She danced round and round till she could hardly stand. But she never danced with any stars, no, not one. For the stars were not there at all. They were nothing more than reflections in the wet grass.

When the little girl realized this, she fell to the ground sobbing. And the fairies stopped their dancing and hovered round her.

'I've swum and I've swum,' she sobbed. 'I've danced and I've danced. And still I have not found the stars.'

The fairies felt sorry for the little girl, so they did what they could. They gave her a little riddle.

'Ask Four Feet to carry you to No Feet At All,' they told her. 'Then ask No Feet At All to carry you to the Stairs Without Steps. And there you will find the stars.'

The fairies went back to their dancing, and the little girl went on her way.

Soon she met a horse.

'Excuse me,' she asked, as politely as she could, 'I'm on my way to the stars. Could you give me a ride?'

The horse neighed and shook his shaggy head. 'I cannot help you,' he explained. 'For

I am here to help the fairies and the fairies only.'

'Ah,' the little girl smiled, 'then you must be Four Feet. The fairies told me about you. They said that I must ask you to take me to No Feet At All.'

'Well, that's different!' the horse snorted. 'Climb aboard, and we shall be there in no time.' And off they went, through the forests and over the fields—hooves hammering and hair blowing, west and west and west, until they reached the sea.

'I can carry you no further,' the horse explained. 'You must wait here on the beach for No Feet At All.'

The little girl had so many questions. Who was No Feet At All? What did he look like? How would she find him? But before she could ask a single question, the horse turned and galloped away. The little girl looked up into the sky. The stars were as far away as ever. And she was lost and all alone.

Suddenly, however, something went splash. Then splish-splash. Then splish-splash-splish. The girl looked into the sea, and there was a fish—a huge fish, a massive fish, a great giant of a fish, with green and yellow scales and the kindest looking grey-green eyes.

'Could it be?' she wondered. And so she called, 'No Feet At All? Is that you, No Feet At All?' And the great fish leaped out of the water and landed near the edge of the beach.

'Where shall I carry you, my dear?' asked the fish.

'To the Stairs Without Steps,' said the little girl. And off they went, fins flapping, night-dress dripping, slicing through the salty waves, west and west and west. And then the fish just stopped.

'We're here,' he gurgled, 'at the Stairs Without Steps.'

But the little girl could see nothing at all.

'Step off my back,' the fish insisted. 'It will be all right.'

So the little girl stepped—stepped off the fish's back and into what looked for all the world like a vast and endless sea. But before her foot could touch the water, a pure white gull flew under it. She stepped higher, and there was another gull, and so she stepped higher still. And with every step, a gull was there to hold her. When she had climbed too high for the gulls to fly, the clouds took over, and step by cloudy step they carried her at last to the land of the stars!

The stars reached out their warm and shiny arms to welcome her, and she spent the rest of that night dancing their sparkling dances and playing their golden games. When the little girl finally grew tired, they wrapped her up in a cloud and sent her off to sleep.

'Come again any time!' the stars said, their eyes twinkling, their faces shining.

The girl dreamed of fairies and night wind and stars. But when she awoke, she was back in her room and the cloud beneath her head was nothing more than her own soft pillow. Had it all been a dream, nothing more than a dream? Then why was the hem of her night-dress damp? And why did her hair smell of cold, salty air? And where had the horsehair come from, which she clutched in her little hand?

The little girl smiled, and pulled the blankets tight up to her chin. Then she made another wish, and shut her eyes, and set off to dream again.

Three Months' Night

The pine trees stood tall. The mountains behind them stood taller still. And, in a clearing in the midst of the trees, the animals gathered together.

Their leader, the coyote, perched on a wide flat rock and howled, 'A-Woo,' so everyone could hear.

'My friends,' he called, 'we have a decision to make. Think hard. Take your time. And then tell me. How long should each day be?'

The animals looked at one another. They grunted and squealed and roared. Such a hard decision! Then they became quiet, and set to thinking.

After a long while, the grizzly bear raised one fat, furry paw and slowly wiggled his four sharp claws.

'I think...' he yawned. 'I think that each day should be three months long. And the same with each night. That way...' he yawned again, 'we could get all the sleep we need.'

The animals were shocked by the bear's answer, and the grunting and squealing and roaring started all over again. But it was the chipmunk who spoke up most loudly.

'Don't be ridiculous!' he chattered. 'If I slept for three months, I would starve to death! I say we keep things just as they are—with one day followed by one night.'

The owl and the weasel and many of the other animals agreed. But the grizzly stood his ground, and soon the woods were filled with the noise of the animals' argument.

'Enough. A-Woo. Enough!' the coyote howled. 'We will settle this matter with a contest. Chipmunk, you must repeat, over and over again, the words, "One day, one night", for that is what you want.

'As for you, Grizzly Bear, you must say, "Three months' day, three months' night" over and over again—for that is what you want. And the first one to say the wrong thing will be the loser. Now clear your throats, take your places, and let the contest begin!'

Chipmunk scurried up into the branches of a tall pine tree. Grizzly Bear settled himself on the ground and leaned against the trunk. And then they started.

'One day, one night, one day, one night,' the chipmunk chattered, faster and faster in his squeaky little voice.

'Three months' day, three months' night,' the bear repeated slowly, but he was sleepy and tired and found it hard to concentrate.

'One day, one night, one day, one night, one day, one night,' the chipmunk chattered faster than ever, and it was all the bear could do to hear his own grizzly voice. And that's when it happened. Instead of saying, 'Three months' day, three months' night,' the poor bear mumbled, 'One day, one night.' And the contest was over!

'Chipmunk has won. A-Woo!' the coyote howled. 'And so it shall be one day and one night forevermore.'

But the grizzly bear refused to give in. 'I need three months' sleep,' he growled, 'and I intend to get it!'

He stood up and swung an angry paw at Chipmunk. But Chipmunk darted away, so that the bear's claws left nothing but four long scratches down his back. Then the bear sulked away, hid himself in a cave, and settled down for a long winter's sleep.

And, to this day, every chipmunk bears the marks of Grizzly's claws on his back. And each winter every grizzly goes to sleep for a three months' night.

Arion and the Dolphin

When Arion played his harp, everybody listened.

The Greek men put down their tools. The Greek women put down their pots. The Greek children put down their toys. And even the birds in the air, the animals in the field, and the fish in the sea stopped their screeching and scratching and splashing to listen to his beautiful songs.

Arion was hardly more than a boy, but no one played the harp more skilfully or sang so sweetly. The king himself had said so! And so it came as no surprise when Arion decided to leave his homeland and sail for the island of Sicily, hoping to find fame and fortune there as well.

It happened, of course.

When Arion played, everybody listened.

The Sicilian men put down their tools. The Sicilian women put down their pots. The Sicilian children put down their toys. And, along with the birds and the fish and the animals, they marvelled at the Greek lad's lovely songs.

The people of Sicily showered Arion with silver and gold and jewels. So it was as a rich young man that he boarded a Greek ship and set sail for home.

The captain of the ship knew all about Arion, but he cared little for music and a great deal for gold. So, when they had sailed far from shore, he made his sailors grab hold of Arion and drag him to the side of the ship.

'You are a rich young man, Arion,' the captain laughed, 'but not for long. My men are going to kill you and throw your body overboard, and we shall have your treasure!'

'Dear captain,' Arion sighed, 'if your heart is set on ending my life and stealing my fortune, there is nothing I can do to stop you. But at least grant me one wish before I die. Let me play my harp one last time.'

The captain shrugged. 'What harm can it do?' And he tossed the musician his harp.

Arion began to play. Arion began to sing. And, just as he expected, everybody listened.

The sailors put down their ropes. The captain put down his sword. Even the gulls above and the fish below stopped their swooping and swimming to listen to the lad's last beautiful song.

But, just as the song was about to finish, Arion grabbed his harp tightly and flung himself from the boat and into the bright blue sea.

'Don't worry about him, lads,' the captain

called. 'No one could swim to shore from here. The sharks will see to that. Now, let's have a look at that treasure!'

Arion, meanwhile, began to sink, for he could not hold on to his harp and swim. Down and down, deeper and deeper, sank the poor singer.

And then, suddenly, he stopped! And instead of sinking further, he began to rise, up and up, higher and higher, until his head popped out of the waves and he could breathe again!

Arion looked down and was surprised to find himself sitting on the back of a dolphin— a dolphin who had heard Arion's beautiful song and was determined that such a singer should not drown.

Arion wrapped his legs round the dolphin's sides. He wrapped one arm round its neck. And the dolphin carried Arion through the waves, all the way back to Greece.

Arion thanked his new friend and waved goodbye. And the dolphin leaped up out of the sea, clapping and clacking his farewell. Then Arion tucked his harp under his arm and set off to see the king.

When he arrived at the palace, the king was busy—in fact, he was talking with the very sailors who had stolen Arion's treasure. So Arion asked the guard to keep silent, while he slipped quietly behind a stone pillar to listen.

'It was a sorry thing, Your Majesty,' the captain explained. 'The storm came upon us like a fierce beast and, before we could do a thing, poor Arion and his treasure were swept overboard.'

The king sadly shook his head. 'I can't believe it,' he sighed. 'I shall never hear that beautiful voice and harp again.'

But just as the king finished, the sound of a harp came floating out from the back of the hall. And it was followed by Arion's beautiful voice.

The guards put down their spears. The king put down his royal staff. And the sailors fell trembling to their knees.

Arion slipped out from behind the pillar and walked slowly towards the throne. The king clapped his hands for joy.

'You're alive!' he shouted. 'You did not drown! What power saved you from the terrible storm?'

'There was no storm, Your Majesty.' Arion explained. And then he told the king all about the captain's wicked plan.

Soldiers were sent to the ship and, sure enough, they found Arion's treasure. So the captain and his crew were packed off to prison. Arion's treasure was returned to him. And the king ordered his sculptors to make a statue of a boy on the back of a dolphin—in memory of Arion and his amazing rescue.

Rabbit and Tiger Save the World

Tiger was huge! Tiger was fierce! Tiger had sharp claws, even sharper teeth, and beautiful orange-and-black striped skin. But, for all his good looks, Tiger was not very clever.

Rabbit, on the other hand, was small. And not very scary at all. Rabbit had long ears, a powder-puff tail and a brain that was every bit as quick as his long, strong legs.

Tiger wanted to eat Rabbit, more than anything else in the world!

And, more than anything else in the world, Rabbit did not want to be eaten!

One day, as Rabbit was out nibbling daisies for his dinner, Tiger surprised him. Tiger chased Rabbit through the jungle and across the fields and into a deep, rocky ravine.

There was no way out. Rabbit was trapped! So he stopped using his quick legs and used his quick brain instead. He threw himself, arms outstretched, against a huge boulder at the end of the ravine, and waited for Tiger to catch up.

'Now I've got you!' Tiger roared. 'And I can almost taste the rabbit stew.'

'You may eat me if you like,' said Rabbit, slowly, 'but first you will have to tear me away from this boulder I am holding up.'

'And what would be wrong with that?' asked the puzzled Tiger.

'Well, this boulder holds up the whole world,' answered Rabbit. 'I saw it start to roll away, and fortunately I was here to stop it. But if I move away from here, it will start rolling again—and take the whole world with it!'

'Oh dear!' said Tiger, 'I had no idea.'

'I'll tell you what,' grinned Rabbit. 'Why don't you hold it up for me and let me run and get some help.'

'Certainly,' said the worried Tiger. 'We don't want the world to roll away!'

So Rabbit ran. But he didn't run for help. He ran straight home to his rabbit hidey-hole, laughing all the way—and safe at last.

The Shepherd and the Clever Princess

Princess Vendla could speak any language. Any language in the world!

German, French.

Italian, Polish.

Chinese, Zulu, English.

She could understand them all.

Her father, the king, was proud of her. So proud, in fact, that he set a challenge for all the young men in his kingdom.

'If you want to marry my daughter,' he announced, 'you must first speak to her in a language she does not understand. Succeed, and she shall be your bride. Fail, and you shall be thrown into the sea!'

Many men tried. Wise men. Rich men. Handsome men. But, sadly, each and every one of them ended up in the sea.

And then, one day, Timo the shepherd boy decided that it was time to find a wife.

'They say the princess is quite pretty,' he thought. 'So I shall take up the king's challenge and make her my bride.'

Now Timo was neither wise, nor rich, nor handsome. In fact, he was a dreamer, who wandered through the forests and across the fields chatting with the birds and whispering to the animals.

Timo set off for the king's palace. He hadn't gone far when he heard a noise—a chippery, chirping noise—the cry of a little bird. But the noise wasn't falling down from somewhere high in the trees. No, it was leaping up from somewhere on the ground.

Timo followed the noise. He brushed away branches and bark and old, dead leaves. And soon he found it—a sad young sparrow with a badly broken wing.

'Poor little fellow,' Timo said. 'You're lucky you haven't been gobbled up by a fox or a cat. Why don't you ride with me for a while?'

And Timo picked up the little sparrow and set him gently in his big leather pouch.

Timo walked a little further and soon he heard another noise—a scritchity, scratching noise that could come only from a squirrel.

'I'm caught. I'm caught in a trap!' the little squirrel chattered. 'Won't somebody please help me?'

Timo was there in a minute. He loosened the sharp wire from around the squirrel's leg. Then he picked him up and put him in his pouch next to the sparrow.

'You can rest there,' he whispered to the squirrel, 'until your leg is better.'

Timo started off for the king's palace, once again, but it wasn't long before he heard yet another noise—a crawing, caw-cawing noise, high above his head.

'What's the matter, Mr Crow?' Timo called.

'I have lost my wife!' cawed the crow. 'The king's hunters were out in the woods, and I fear they have taken her. I have been flying in circles for hours and I cannot find her.'

'Why not come with me?' said Timo. 'I am going to the king's palace this very day. You can hop into my pouch and ride along.'

The tired crow gladly accepted Timo's offer, and before long, the shepherd boy and his secret companions were at the palace gates.

'Who goes there?' shouted the watchman.

'It's Timo, the shepherd boy. I have come to marry the princess.'

'You mean you've come to be tossed into the sea!' the watchman laughed. 'Men wiser and richer than yourself have found their way there already.'

'Perhaps,' Timo nodded. 'But they did not know what I know—a language that Princess Vendla will not understand.'

The watchman let Timo into the palace, and then led him to the king.

'Your Majesty,' Timo bowed, 'I have come to take up your challenge. I believe I know a language that your daughter will not understand.'

The king could not keep himself from laughing.

'But you are just a poor shepherd boy,' he chuckled. 'And my daughter has studied every language in the world! The sea is very cold at this time of year. Are you sure you want to accept my challenge?'

'I do,' Timo nodded. 'I want to see the princess.'

The king called for his daughter, and she was the most beautiful girl young Timo had ever seen. He bowed to the princess, then he reached his hand into his leather pouch and gently scratched the little sparrow's head.

'Chip-chirp-chippery-chirp,' said the sparrow.

Timo looked at Princess Vendla. 'Can you tell me what that means?' he asked.

Princess Vendla looked very worried. 'Why, no,' she said slowly, 'I can't.'

'It means: "Thank you for rescuing me, Timo. My wing is much better now."'

Timo reached his hand into his pouch again, and this time he tickled the squirrel under his furry chin.

'Scrick-scrack-scrickity-scrack,' said the squirrel. And again the princess could only shake her head.

'This is an easy one,' said Timo. 'It means: "Thank you for the ride and for saving me from the hunter's trap."'

Timo reached his hand once more into his pouch, but before he could nudge the crow,

the king stood up and shouted, 'Enough! I am ashamed of you, daughter. I gave you the finest teachers in the world and yet this ignorant shepherd boy knows more than you!'

'I'm sorry, Father,' the princess sobbed, 'perhaps I am not so clever as you thought.'

'Oh no, princess,' said Timo. 'You are very clever indeed. Clever enough to admit that there are things you still must learn. That is the beginning of real wisdom, and I admire you all the more for it.'

The king smiled when he heard these words. He announced that Timo and Vendla should be married that very day, and everyone in the palace cheered.

So it was that Timo came to live at the palace. And, with the help of the sparrow, the squirrel, the crows, and all his other woodland friends, he taught Princess Vendla the language of the animals.

And they all lived happily ever after.

Tortoise Brings Food

The sun was hot. The earth was dry. There had been no rain for many months. And now there was no food. The animals were very hungry.

Lion, king of all the beasts, called his thin and tired friends together under the shade of a tall, gnarled tree.

'The legends say this is a magic tree,' he roared, 'which will give us all the food we need—if only we can say its secret name. But there is only one person who knows that name—the old man who lives at the top of the mountain.'

'Then we must go to him,' trumpeted Elephant, 'as quickly as we can! Before we all starve to death.'

'I'll go,' said Tortoise, slowly. And everyone just stopped and stared.

'Don't be silly,' roared Lion. 'It would take you for ever! No, we shall send Hare to find the name of the tree. He will be back in no time.'

Hare hurried up the side of the mountain, his long ears blown back against the side of his head. He leaped. He scampered. He raced. And soon he was face to face with the old man.

'Please tell me the name of the magic tree,' he begged. 'The animals are very hungry.'

The old man looked. The old man listened. And then the old man said one word and one word only: 'Uwungelema.'

'Thank you,' panted Hare. And then he hurried back down the mountainside.

He leaped. He scampered. He raced. All the while repeating to himself the name of the magic tree: 'Uwungelema, Uwungelema, Uwungelema.'

But, just as he reached the bottom of the mountain, Hare hurried—CRASH!—right into the side of a huge anthill, and knocked himself silly.

So silly, in fact, that by the time he had staggered back to all the other animals, he

had completely forgotten the name of the magic tree!

'We must send someone else,' roared Lion. 'Someone who will not forget.'

'I'll go,' said Tortoise, again.

And this time, the other animals laughed.

'We'll have starved to death by the time you get back,' chuckled Lion. 'No, we shall send Elephant.'

Elephant hurried up the side of the mountain, his long trunk swaying back and forth. He tramped. He trundled. He tromped. And soon he was face to face with the old man.

'Please tell me the name of the magic tree,' he begged. 'The animals are very hungry.'

The old man looked puzzled. 'I have already told Hare,' he said. 'But I suppose I can tell you, too.' And then he said that word: 'Uwungelema.'

'Thank you,' panted Elephant. And then he hurried back down the mountainside.

He tramped. He trundled. He tromped. All the while repeating to himself that secret name: 'Uwungelema, Uwungelema, Uwungelema.' But, just like Hare, he was in such a hurry that he failed to notice the anthill. And he too stumbled—CRASH!—right into its side, knocking himself so silly that he, too, forgot the secret name.

'This is ridiculous!' roared Lion. 'Is there no one who can remember a simple name?'

'I can,' said Tortoise, quietly.

And the other animals just shook their heads.

'Enough!' roared Lion. 'It looks as if I shall have to do this myself.'

So Lion hurried up the hill and talked to the old man. But on the way back he, too, stumbled into the anthill and staggered back to the others, having forgotten the name completely.

'What shall we do now?' moaned Giraffe.

'I will go,' said Tortoise, determined to help. And before anyone could say anything, he started up the mountain.

He did not hurry, for that is not the tortoise way. Instead, he toddled. He trudged. He took one small step at a time. And, finally, he reached the old man.

'Please tell me the name of the magic tree,' he said slowly, 'for my friends are very hungry.'

The old man looked angrily at Tortoise. 'I have already given the name to Hare, to Elephant and to Lion. I will say it one more time. But if you cannot remember it, I will not say it again!'

And then he spoke the word: 'Uwungelema.'

'Thank you,' said Tortoise, as politely as he could. 'I promise you that I will not forget.' And he started back down the mountain.

He toddled. He trudged. He took one small

step at a time, all the while slowly repeating, 'Uwungelema, Uwungelema, Uwungelema.' And when he came to the anthill, he simply wandered round it. For he was in no hurry. No hurry at all.

When he returned, the animals huddled round him.

'Do you know the name?' they asked. 'Did you remember it?'

'Of course,' Tortoise smiled. 'It's not hard at all.' Then he looked at the magic tree and said the word: 'Uwungelema.'

Immediately, sweet, ripe fruit burst out from the magic tree's branches and fell to the ground before the hungry animals. They hollered. They cheered. They ate till they were full—that day and the next and all through the terrible famine.

And, when the famine was over, they made Tortoise their new king. And they never laughed at him again.

Polly and the Frog

Polly had a very wicked stepmother. Her own mother had died when Polly was just a little girl. And the woman her father had married did not like Polly. Not one little bit. So she made Polly do the hardest jobs around the house. And if Polly did not do them perfectly, she was punished. As for Polly's father, he loved the woman so much that he would do nothing to stop her.

One day, the wicked stepmother called for Polly. And, very sternly, she said, 'Girl,' (for she never called Polly by name) 'take this sieve to the well, fill it with water, and bring it straight back to me.'

Polly knew this was impossible! For the sieve was full of holes and she could never fill it with water. No one could!

Polly said nothing. She just nodded her head and walked slowly to the well. But when she got there, all she could do was plonk herself down at the side of the well and weep.

'Bar-durp,' came a voice from inside the well. 'Bar-durp. Bar-durp.'

Polly wiped her eyes on her sleeve and looked down into the well.

And there was a frog—the biggest, fattest, friendliest frog she had ever seen.

'Bar-durp,' said the frog again. 'You don't look very happy, young lady. Can you tell me what's the matter?'

'It's my stepmother,' Polly sniffled, forgetting all those warnings about never talking to strange frogs. 'She wants me to fill this sieve with water. It's impossible, I know, but if I don't do it she'll punish me the minute I get home.'

'It's not impossible at all!' the frog bar-durped. 'I'll tell you how to do it, if you'll promise me one thing.'

'Anything!' Polly sobbed.

'You must do everything I ask of you for one whole night! Bar-durp.'

Well, it seemed a strange thing to ask, but Polly was desperate. And besides, this frog didn't even know where she lived.

'All right,' Polly agreed. 'Now tell me, please.'

'Bar-durp. Take some moss and some old leaves and jam them into the holes. Then the water won't leak out.'

Polly did what the frog suggested and, sure enough, it worked!

'Thank you!' she smiled. 'You've saved my life!'

'Bar-durp,' the frog smiled back. 'Just remember your promise.' And he did a fat bellyflop back into the water.

Polly hurried home, and her stepmother was so amazed that, for once, she didn't even try to find something wrong with Polly's work. But, later that night, as Polly was finishing her dinner, there was a knock at the door.

'Polly,' her father called. 'There's a frog here to see you.'

Polly swallowed the mouthful of food she was chewing, then rose slowly and walked to the front door. The fat, friendly frog was dripping all over the front mat.

'So it's Polly, is it?' croaked the frog. 'Nice name. Do you mind if I—bar-durp—come in?'

Polly minded very much. But she also remembered her promise. So she invited him in, and then added, very quickly, 'But we're in the middle of dinner.'

'Oh that's all right,' the frog said, flicking out his fat tongue, 'I could do with a snack, myself. Bar-durp.'

Polly returned to the dining-room with the frog hopping happily behind her. At first, her stepmother looked angry, and then a wicked smile slithered across her face. This was the perfect opportunity to make fun of her pretty stepdaughter.

'Oh, I see you've found a new friend?' she sneered. 'He seems a perfect match for you.'

'Bar-durp,' said the frog. 'It's very hard to see down here. Could I hop onto your lap?'

What could Polly do? She had promised. So she picked the frog up (he was very slimy!) and put him on her lap.

The stepmother laughed. She giggled. She guffawed. This was very funny indeed.

Then the frog made his next request.

'Your food smells very good. Bar-durp. Do you think I could have a bite?'

The stepmother was howling now. 'Yes, yes!' she laughed. 'Let's see you feed your little froggy friend!'

Polly sighed and shook her head. Then she scooped up a bit of her dinner and fed it to the frog.

'MMMM,' said the frog. 'Delicious. Bar-durp.'

'Perhaps the froggy would like a drink, as well,' the stepmother teased.

'No, thank you,' the frog croaked. 'But I do have one more request. I wonder if Polly would kiss me—right here on the cheek!'

The stepmother coughed, then choked, then shrieked with laughter.

Polly turned bright red.

'I thought you were my friend,' she whispered to the frog.

'I am. Bar-durp. Trust me—friends keep their promises.'

'So they do,' sighed Polly. And she shut her eyes and kissed the frog on his green, slimy cheek...

But when Polly opened her eyes, the frog was gone! And in his place sat the most handsome young man she had ever seen!

'You've done it!' he shouted, leaping off her lap and dancing for joy. 'You've broken the curse and now I'm free again! Will you come with me to my castle tonight and be my princess?'

Polly looked at her father and her step-mother. Her father looked amazed and the wicked stepmother was no longer laughing.

'Yes,' she said at last. 'Yes, I will. I think I would like that very much. But what about them?'

'Well,' said the prince, as he stared at the stepmother, 'we do have a great many wells and a kitchen full of sieves. I suppose we could use the help.'

'No, please don't worry,' the stepmother muttered. 'We'll stay right here.'

'Yes,' her father agreed. 'You two young people go off and enjoy yourselves.'

And so they did. Polly married the prince. They went to live in his castle. And the girl who kept her promise to a fat, friendly frog lived happily ever after. Bar-durp.

Rabbit and Tiger Go Fishing

It was late, very late, and Rabbit sat by the side of the river, fishing. A night breeze blew. The river rippled gently by. And the moon shone in the water like a bright, white ball.

Suddenly, Tiger burst through the jungle leaves and breathed hot and heavy down Rabbit's back!

'I've got you now!' he growled. 'There is no way you can escape.'

Rabbit trembled. Perhaps this time Tiger was right. And then he saw the moon's reflection in the water, and he had an idea.

'Oh dear,' he muttered, 'you've come at a very bad time, Tiger. Do you see that cheese in the water, there? I was just about to pull it up from the bottom.' And he pointed at the reflection of the moon!

Now if there was anything that Tiger liked to eat more than rabbit, it was cheese.

'Let me have that!' he growled again. And he snatched the fishing-rod from Rabbit's paws. But when he pulled up the line, there was nothing on it.

'See what you've done!' Rabbit scolded. 'In your hurry, you let the cheese get away. But I can still see it down there. Perhaps if you were to dive in and grab it with your big strong claws...'

'Excellent!' Tiger roared. 'And when I return I shall have rabbit and cheese for supper tonight!'

So into the water he jumped. And, as soon as Tiger went 'SPLASH!', Rabbit scampered home.

He got free.
He got safe.
He got clean away.
And all Tiger got was... wet.

The Mouse Deer's Wisdom

Once there lived a baker—a fat and wealthy baker—who baked the best cakes in the land. But this baker—this fat and wealthy baker—had a problem. So he went to see the king.

'Your Majesty,' the baker explained, 'I have a problem. Next to my bakery, there is a little house. And in that little house there lives a little family—a mother, a father and two small children. They are poor, to be sure, but for many years now, day after day, they have

freely enjoyed the privilege of smelling my wonderful cakes. Do you not think that they owe me just a little money for that pleasure?'

The king stroked his beard and thought. This was a difficult question, indeed. So he called his wise men and his magicians and his advisers and shared the problem with them. And soon they were stroking their beards too. No one had an answer.

'I know what we must do,' the king said finally, 'we must send for the Mouse Deer!'

The Mouse Deer—who lived in the jungle near the king's palace—was by far the wisest creature in the land. He had to be, you see, for he was also one of the smallest and would have been eaten up long ago were it not for his wisdom and wit.

One of the king's advisers was sent to fetch the Mouse Deer and tell him the baker's problem.

The Mouse Deer came at once. He bowed to the king. Then he grinned a sly grin, and said, 'Your Majesty, I have considered the baker's problem with great care. And now I have an answer: the baker must be paid!'

The surprised advisers looked at each other.

But the baker could only smile.

'What is more,' the Mouse Deer continued, 'because even the smell of his wonderful cakes is a pleasure fit for a king, the baker must be paid a king's reward—a thousand silver pieces!'

The astonished advisers' jaws dropped. But it was all the baker could do to keep from dancing.

'Sadly,' the Mouse Deer concluded, 'this poor family cannot afford such a great sum. So I shall pay the baker myself—right here in court—if Your Majesty would be so kind as to lend me the money.'

The king stroked his beard again. He did not know what the little animal was up to, but he trusted him. So he told his treasurer to fetch a thousand silver pieces.

When the big bag of coins arrived, the Mouse Deer asked everyone to be seated.

'We need to be sure it's all here,' he said. And the Mouse Deer began to count.

'One silver piece,' he counted. Then he threw it on the marble floor so it rang like a little silver bell.

'Two silver pieces,' he counted. And that one rang against the floor as well.

'Three, four, five silver pieces,' he went on, throwing each one to the floor. And so he continued, all the way to a thousand, until the whole room rang with the jingling and the jangling of the coins.

When the Mouse Deer had finally finished, the baker jumped out of his seat, eager to scoop up his treasure. But, before he could pick up even one piece, the Mouse Deer raised a tiny hoof.

'Wait just a minute,' he said. 'There is no need for you to pick up these coins, for you have been paid already!'

The baker stopped and stared.

The king scratched his head.

The advisers all said, 'Huh?'

And so the Mouse Deer explained, 'You say that poor family owed you money for the pleasure of smelling your cakes, even though they never got to taste a single crumb. I say that I have paid you in the very same way. For, although you will never be able to spend even one of these silver coins, you have had the pleasure of hearing them being counted. Hearing the coins for smelling the cakes—it seems a fair trade to me.'

The baker turned to the king in anger, but all the king could do was smile.

'It seems a fair trade to me, as well,' he said. Then, without a smile, he added, 'From now on, that poor family could do with less of your greed and more of your kindness.'

The baker lowered his head and bowed. Then he slipped sheepishly out of the palace, never to return.

The advisers applauded, the magicians marvelled, and the wise men cheered, 'Hooray!'

And the Mouse Deer returned to his home in the jungle, still the wisest creature in all the land!

The Four Friends

It was evening. The long, hot day was over. And the four friends gathered by the water-hole.

'Good evening to you all,' called Raven, high in the branches of a tree.

'I hope everyone is well,' chirped Rat, as he crawled out of his hole in the muddy bank.

'Very well, indeed,' yawned Turtle, as he floated lazily to the water's surface.

'And very happy to be among friends,' added Goat, as she bent down to take a drink.

The four friends talked and laughed and played by the water's edge. Then they went their separate ways for the night, promising to return the next evening.

But when the next evening came, someone was missing.

'Greetings, one and all,' called Raven, high in the branches of a tree.

'And how is everyone tonight?' chirped Rat, as he crawled out of his hole in the muddy bank.

'Very well, indeed,' yawned Turtle, as he floated lazily to the water's surface. But when it was time for Goat to speak, Goat was not there!

'Perhaps she's late,' called Raven, flying down to join the others.

'Perhaps she's with her family,' suggested Rat, pacing back and forth in front of his hole.

'Perhaps she's met the Hunter!' cried Turtle, as he pulled his worried face deep into his shell.

'Well, if that's the case,' said Raven, 'I must go and look for her. We're four friends, right? And we have promised always to help each other.'

So off Raven flew, high above the jungle.

He looked left and he looked right.

He looked high and he looked low.

And finally he found what he was looking for—his friend Goat, trapped in the Hunter's net.

'Help me. Please help me!' Goat cried. 'The Hunter has gone off to check his other nets, but when he returns he will kill me.'

Faster than he had ever flown before, Raven darted back to the water-hole.

'This may hurt a little,' he explained to Rat. 'I am going to pick you up with my claws and carry you to Goat. She is trapped in the Hunter's net and only your sharp teeth can set her free.'

So Raven grabbed Rat with his sharp claws and carried him over the trees to Goat.

Rat had never been so frightened. But when he saw his poor friend, he forgot all about his fear, and set to gnawing through the net.

Turtle, meanwhile, swam back and forth impatiently across the water-hole.

'My friend is in trouble,' he muttered to himself, 'and I must do what I can to help.'

So he climbed out of the water-hole and trundled slowly across the jungle floor, in the direction that Raven had flown.

'Hurry!' cried Raven, watching carefully for the Hunter's return. 'He could be back any minute!'

'I'm chewing as fast as I can,' mumbled Rat through a

mouthful of net. 'But these ropes are strong.'

Raven watched.

Rat chewed.

Goat strained against the net and finally, with a SNAP, she was free!

Just then, there came a rustling noise from the bushes behind them. The three friends froze with fear!

'Hello, everyone,' puffed Turtle, breathlessly. 'What can I do to help?'

'Turtle!' cried Raven. 'What are you doing here?'

'We've already set Goat free,' Rat explained. 'And now it's time for us to run.'

'But you are so slow,' moaned Goat. 'However will you get away?'

'We'll find out soon enough,' announced Raven, 'for here comes the Hunter!'

The Hunter burst through the under-growth, and the four friends set off in all directions. Raven took to the air. Rat scurried under a log. Goat raced off across the jungle. But all poor Turtle could do was pull in his legs and hope that the Hunter would not see him.

The Hunter, however, had far better eyesight than that.

'The goat is gone!' he sighed. 'But never mind, here is a nice fat turtle, just right for my dinner.' And he picked up Turtle and dropped him into his hunter's sack.

Raven watched it all, and flew off to fetch Goat. He whispered a plan in her ear and, even before he had finished, she agreed, 'I'll do it!'

Then, instead of running even farther away from the Hunter, she ran right towards him. He spotted her at once, and the chase began.

Goat was too fast for him. Far too fast. The Hunter threw down his big stick. He threw off his coat. And at last he threw down the sack that held Turtle—all to gain more speed.

'I'll be back for you later!' he shouted. And he hurried after Goat, who led him far away from Turtle before making her escape.

Meanwhile Raven found Rat, and the two of them chopped and chewed away at the sack until there was a hole big enough for Turtle to wriggle out.

The next evening, the four friends gathered, as usual, at the water-hole.

'Good evening to you all!' called Raven, high in the branches of a tree.

'And how is everyone,' chirped Rat, 'after our great adventure?'

'Very well indeed,' yawned Turtle. 'Happy to be alive!'

'And happier than ever,' added Goat, 'to be among friends!'

The Brave Bull Calf

Once upon a time, there lived a boy—a boy who owned a baby bull. They raced and they wrestled. They butted and they kicked. They did everything together. They were the very best of friends.

But the boy grew. And the baby bull did too. Until, one day, the boy's wicked stepfather announced that it was time to take the bull to market.

The boy was horrified. And so, that very night, he set off with the bull—to save his friend's life and to seek his fortune.

They walked for a night and a day, through forests and towns and fields. And, at the end of the day, the boy begged a loaf of bread from a friendly old farmer.

'Here you go,' he said to the bull. 'Half for you and half for me.'

'You have it all,' the bull snorted. 'I am happy just to chew on a little grass.'

'Oh no,' said the boy. 'We are friends, and always will be. And friends share whatever they have.'

The next day was much the same. They walked through fields and towns and forests. And at the end of the day, they begged a chunk of cheese from a tired little tinker.

'Here you go,' said the boy to the bull.

'Half for you and half for me.'

'You have it all,' the bull said again. 'I am happy just to munch on a bit of clover.'

'Oh no,' the boy said. 'We are friends, and always will be. And friends share whatever they have.'

On the third day, they walked farther still, through fields and forests and towns. And at the end of the day, they begged a fresh turnip from a short, stout shopkeeper.

'Here you go,' said the boy again. 'Half for you and half for me.'

But this time the bull said nothing.

'What's the matter?' asked the boy. 'You've been quiet all day long.'

'I had a dream last night,' whispered the bull. 'A sad and scary dream. Tomorrow we will not walk through forests and fields and towns. We will wander into the wild woods. We will meet a tiger, a leopard, and a dragon. I will fight the first two and defeat them. And then I will fight the dragon—and he will kill me.'

'No!' cried the boy, wrapping his arms around the bull's neck. 'That will not happen! I won't let it!'

'But you must,' said the bull. 'For that is the only way you will find your fortune. When I am dead, you must cut off my right horn. It will be more powerful than ever, then. And you can use it to kill the dragon.'

'No!' said the boy. 'I won't!'

'But you must,' said the bull again. 'For you are my friend, and always will be. And friends share whatever they have.'

Neither the boy nor the bull slept well that night. And the next morning they walked, step by sorry step, towards the wild woods.

'This is the place,' said the bull, at last. 'The place I saw in my dream. Now climb this tree. Climb high and hide yourself. And I will do my best to protect you.'

The boy had hardly reached the top, when the tiger appeared, eyes flashing and sharp teeth bared.

The bull snorted. The tiger roared. And soon they were fighting for their lives. But the bull's huge horns and sharp hooves proved too much for the tiger, and before long, he limped away into the woods.

The bull hardly had time to lick his wounds when the leopard appeared. The bull bellowed. The leopard growled. But he was no match for the bull, either. He spat and he clawed and he bit. But in the end he crept away, beaten and bruised, just like the tiger.

The boy was about to holler, 'Hooray!' when he felt the tree shake beneath him. And not just the tree, but the ground below as well.

And that's when the dragon appeared, mouth flaming, tail slashing, as tall as a tree himself!

The bull snorted and pawed and rushed at the monster, but it was no use. The dragon raised its long neck, lashed out with its giant claw, and the poor bull fell to the ground. Fell to rise no more.

The dragon shook its scaly head and roared, then lumbered away into the woods. And when he had gone, the boy climbed down from the tree and wept over his dead friend.

'I will not forget you,' he vowed, as he cut off the bull's right horn. 'I will use this horn, just as you said. I promise to make you proud of me.'

With the horn tucked in his belt, the boy set off through the wild woods. He walked sadly. He walked carefully, ready to fight off any enemy he might find. But all he found was a girl—a beautiful girl—tied to an old oak tree.

'Help me!' the girl cried. 'Please help me! My father, the king, has left me here to be eaten by the dragon. He says it's the only way to stop the monster attacking our town.'

The boy was sorry for the princess, but just as he was untying her he felt the ground shake once more. And, with a flash of his tail and a fiery roar, the dragon appeared!

The princess screamed. The boy wanted to scream, too. And to run away as far as he could. But he remembered his friend's dream, and what his friend had died for. So he ran straight at the dragon, as fast as he could.

Just as the dragon reached out to maul him, he drove the point of the bull's horn into the soft sole of the dragon's foot, and the dragon fell down dead!

The boy pulled the horn out of the dragon's foot, and then finished untying the princess.

'What's going on here?' came a deep voice from the woods. It was the king. 'I ordered you to stay here!' the king said to the princess.

'To save our people from the dragon.'

'But Father,' the girl explained, 'this boy has already done that. He has killed the dragon and saved our people—and me as well!'

'Excellent!' shouted the king. 'Then he must have a reward. What say we give him your hand in marriage? And my throne when I am gone?'

The boy looked at the princess. The princess looked at the boy. It seemed a good idea to both of them—so they were married. And when the time came for him to be king, he ordered a new coat of arms decorated with a tree on one corner, a fallen dragon on the other—and, in the middle, the head of a bull with one horn.

Tiger Gets Stuck

One day, quite by accident, Tiger stumbled across Rabbit's hidey-hole.

He wanted to roar for joy, but decided instead to keep very quiet, and watch and wait for Rabbit to leave.

When, at last, Rabbit hopped away into the jungle, Tiger bounded over to the hole and peered down inside. He knew exactly what he wanted to do.

Tiger slipped one front paw down into the hole. And then he slipped in the other. Next he squeezed his head in, and his shoulders, and his long, striped body. Finally he pulled in his powerful back legs. And he grinned.

'I will wait in here,' Tiger chuckled. 'I will wait very quietly. And when Rabbit comes home, I will gobble him up!'

Unfortunately, Tiger had forgotten something. Something that Rabbit saw the minute he got close to home. Tiger forgot that his tail was still sticking out of the hole—waving a warning like a black-and-orange striped flag!

'Hmmm,' thought Rabbit. 'It looks as if I have a visitor.'

And so he called, 'Hey, Hidey-hole! Ho, Hidey-hole! Are you happy, Hidey-hole?'

Tiger (who still had no idea where his tail was) looked worried.

'Rabbit is talking to his hidey-hole,' he thought. 'I must keep very quiet indeed.'

But just then, Rabbit called again, 'Hey, Hidey-hole! Ho, Hidey-hole! Are you happy, Hidey-hole?'

'Oh dear,' thought Tiger. 'What if Rabbit suspects something is wrong? Perhaps I should answer, after all.'

So the next time Rabbit called, 'Hey, Hidey-hole! Ho, Hidey-hole! Are you happy, Hidey-hole?', Tiger called back, 'Yes, Mr Rabbit, I am very happy, indeed!'

But he said it in such a ridiculous, squeaky little voice that Rabbit could not keep from laughing.

'You silly Tiger,' he called. 'Hidey-holes don't talk! And they don't have long, striped tails sticking out of them either! It looks as if I've tricked you again.'

'Oh no, you haven't,' Tiger growled, 'for now I will come out and eat you!'

But the minute Tiger tried to back himself out of the hidey-hole, he discovered that he was stuck! He scrunched and stretched and squeezed. He wrestled and wriggled and roared. But no amount of moving could get him out.

'Wait right there,' chuckled Rabbit, 'and I will fetch some help. That is, if you promise never to visit my home again.'

'I do,' Tiger whined, for he very much wanted to get out.

So Rabbit fetched Crocodile. And Crocodile clamped his sharp teeth round Tiger's tail. And, after much huffing and puffing and pulling, Tiger came out with a 'pop!' and ran off, embarrassed, into the jungle.

Tiger kept his promise and never came back to Rabbit's home.

And Rabbit never again went home without asking his hidey-hole if it was happy or not.

The Clever Mouse

Many years ago, in a little Welsh town, there was a famine. There was no food anywhere. And everyone—from the richest lord to the poorest peasant—was tired and thin and hungry.

One day, a monk named Cadog came to visit the town. Cadog was good and gentle and kind. He loved God. He loved God's creatures. And he loved to read and write and learn. In fact, that was why he had come to the town—to study under a wise and famous teacher.

'You may be my student,' the teacher promised, 'but I must warn you. There is a famine in these parts, so I have nothing to feed you.'

Cadog didn't mind. Not one bit. He studied hard, day after day at his little desk. And every day he had a visitor—a tiny visitor with fine, grey whiskers, a pointed nose, and a long, pink tail. He climbed on Cadog's desk, and scurried across his books, and scampered over his pile of goose-quill pens.

But Cadog didn't mind. Not one bit. He liked the little mouse and refused to chase him away. And perhaps that is why, one day, the little mouse arrived with a gift.

He climbed onto Cadog's desk. He scampered over Cadog's pens. And, in the middle of Cadog's book, he dropped one yellow grain of wheat!

'Thank you, my friend,' said Cadog to the mouse.

And the mouse sat up and squeaked, as if to say, 'You're welcome.'

Half an hour later he returned with another piece of wheat and Cadog thanked him again.

Soon, the mouse returned a third time. Then a fourth. And a fifth. And a sixth. And when there were finally seven golden grains of wheat lying on his book, Cadog had an idea.

He took a long piece of silken thread and

gently tied one end around the mouse's leg.

'This won't hurt at all,' he promised. 'And it may do a world of good.' Then he let the mouse go and watched to see where it would run. The mouse was much too fast for Cadog, of course, but by following the silken thread he was able to trace the mouse's path—into a hole in the wall, out the other side, across the garden, through the woods, and into a huge earthen mound.

Cadog ran to fetch his teacher, and together they dug into the mound. Buried deep within were the ruins of an old house. And buried deep in the cellar of that old house was an enormous pile of wheat!

Cadog and his teacher ran to tell their friends. And soon the town was filled with the smell of freshly baked bread. Now there was plenty of food for everyone!

The next day, the little mouse came to visit, as usual. He climbed onto Cadog's desk. He scampered over Cadog's pens.

And when he sat down in the middle of Cadog's book, the monk gently untied the silken thread.

'Thank you, my friend,' he said. 'God sent you to me for a reason. And now we know what it was. Your keen nose and tiny feet have saved the entire town.'

Then he tore off a chunk of fresh, warm bread, and set it before the little creature. And the mouse and the monk shared a meal together.

The Amazing Pine Cone

When the old man wandered into town, no one paid attention. He tipped his tattered cap. He waved his wrinkled hand. But everyone ignored him, for he looked just like a beggar.

When the old man wandered through town, he tottered up the hill to the mayor's house. The house was big and bright and beautiful. It was the finest house in town by far. The old man raised his gnarled cane and rapped on the front door.

'What do you want?' called the mayor's wife, as she eased the door open and peered through the gap.

'A place to stay,' the man replied, 'to rest for just one night.'

The mayor's wife looked at the old man. She looked at his tattered cap. She looked at his shabby coat. And she quickly shut the door.

'Go away!' she shouted. 'We have no room for beggars here!'

The old man wandered back through town. He tipped his tattered cap. He waved his wrinkled hand. And still no one paid any attention. He came, at last, to another house—a poor, pathetic, little place. And he rapped on the door with his cane.

A poor, little woman answered the door. And when she saw the old man and his beggar's clothes, she felt sorry for him.

'How can I help you?' she asked.

'I need a place to stay,' said the old man again, 'to rest for just one night.'

'Of course!' she smiled. And she welcomed him into her home.

Next morning, the old man rose early, but before he said goodbye, he reached into his pocket with his wrinkled hand.

'I want to give you something,' he said to the woman. 'It is my way of saying thank you.'

And he handed the woman a pine cone!

The woman didn't know what to say. No one had ever given her a pine cone before. So she smiled as politely as she could, and tried very hard not to giggle.

'This is no ordinary pine cone,' the old man explained. 'It is a magic pine cone. And it will multiply by a thousand times the first thing you do today!'

The woman smiled again. She liked the old man. She appreciated his kindness. But this was the strangest thing she had ever heard.

She said goodbye, and when the old man had gone, she turned to a piece of cloth she had woven the night before. She pulled it out of the basket to fold it, but the more she pulled out and the more she folded, the more cloth there was! Soon, not only her living-room, but her kitchen and her bedroom and the whole of the house was filled with brand new cloth.

The woman shook her head, amazed. So it really was a magic pine cone after all! And it wasn't long before the whole town learned of the woman's good fortune and the old man's magical gift.

Exactly one year later, the old man wandered into the town again. This time no one ignored him. He tipped his tattered cap.

He waved his wrinkled hand. And everyone stopped and smiled and invited him to spend the night.

But, just as he had done before, he wandered through the town to the top of the hill, and knocked on the mayor's door.

The mayor's wife welcomed him with open arms. She gave him the nicest room and the most comfortable bed, and she cooked him a delicious meal.

And as soon as he had gone to bed, she put a pile of gold coins on the table, ready to be counted the moment she received his thank-you gift.

Next morning, just as she had expected, the old man reached into his pocket and handed her a pine cone.

'This is no ordinary pine cone,' he explained. 'It is a magic pine cone. And it will multiply by a thousand times the first thing you do today.'

The mayor's wife nodded and smiled. She could hardly wait for the old man to go. And, as soon as she had shut the door behind him, she raced to the table, ready to count her gold. But before she got there, something happened. Something she had not expected.

The mayor's wife sneezed. And because that was the first thing she did, she sneezed not once, not twice, but a thousand times—for the rest of that day, and the next, and the one after that!

The whole town heard of it, of course. News even reached the old man, who smiled and patted his pocketful of pine cones, and then wandered off to another town, tipping his tattered cap, waving his wrinkled hand, and looking for somewhere to spend the night.

The Very Strong Sparrow

'Too-tweet! Too-tweet! Too-tweet!' the baby birds cried out for their mother.

'Patience, patience,' said Sparrow. 'I've got food enough for everyone here.' And she fed them and hugged them, then wrapped her wings around them. And soon they were fast asleep.

KA-THOOM! KA-THOOM! KA-THOOM!

Elephant came tramping through the jungle. The earth shook. The trees shook. And so did poor Sparrow's nest.

'Too-tweet! Too-tweet! Too-tweet!' cried the baby birds. They were startled, and frightened, and wide awake!

Sparrow was furious. 'See what you've done!' she complained to Elephant. 'You woke up my babies with your tramping and your tromping and your trumpeting. Could you try to be a little quieter?'

KA-THOOM! KA-THOOM! KA-THOOM!

Elephant tramped over to Sparrow's tree.

'Who do you think you're talking to?' he demanded. 'You are nothing but a tiny little sparrow. I am Elephant—the strongest animal in the jungle. And I will do whatever I please.'

'The strongest animal in the jungle? I don't believe it,' said Sparrow. And then, without thinking, she added, 'Why, even I could beat a big bully like you.'

Elephant tossed his trunk in the air and gave a trumpet blast. He had never been so insulted. 'Meet me tomorrow at noon, at the old banana tree,' he roared. 'We will have a test of strength and see who is the strongest animal in the jungle.' Then he tramped away, angry: KA-THOOM! KA-THOOM! KA-THOOM!

'What have I done?' thought Sparrow. 'Well, I had to do something. He was waking up my babies, after all.'

Later that day, Sparrow flew to the river, to take a bath and to fetch some water for her children. But just as she landed at the water's edge, Crocodile appeared.

KER-SPLASH! KER-SPLASH! KER-SPLASH!

He thrashed his scaly tail back and forth

across the water till Sparrow thought she was going to drown.

'Stop it!' she cried. 'All I want is a little water for myself and my babies.'

'Who do you think you're talking to?' snapped Crocodile. 'You are nothing but a tiny little sparrow. And I am Crocodile—the strongest animal in the jungle. And I will do whatever I please.'

Sparrow had heard this before, and she was about to fly away, when she had an idea.

'The strongest animal in the jungle?' she laughed. 'I don't believe it. I will meet you here, tomorrow, just after noon. And I will show you that I am more powerful than you can ever hope to be.'

Crocodile laughed so hard, there were tears in his eyes.

'I'll take you up on that,' he chuckled. 'And if you win, you may drink from my river whenever you like.'

The next day, as the sun reached the top of the sky, Sparrow met Elephant by the old banana tree. She had the end of a long, thick vine in her beak.

'For our test of strength,' she said, 'we shall have a tug of war. You hold this end of the vine, and I will fly off and grab hold of the other end. And when I cry "Pull!" we shall see who is the strongest.'

KA-THOOM! KA-THOOM! KA-THOOM!

Elephant tramped up and down with joy. He could win this contest easily! So he took the vine from Sparrow and she flew off to grab the other end.

But when she picked up the other end, she did not cry "Pull!". At least, not straightaway. No, she carried the vine to the river, where Crocodile was waiting.

KER-SPLASH! KER-SPLASH! KER-SPLASH!

'So you've come after all,' he sneered.

'Yes,' she said. 'And I've come to win! We shall have a tug of war. You take this end, and I will fly off and grab the other end. And when I cry "Pull!" we shall see who is the strongest.'

Crocodile chuckled and clamped his teeth onto the end of the vine. Then Sparrow flew to the middle of the vine—to a spot where she could hear both Elephant and Crocodile, but where they could not hear each other. And that's when she cried, 'PULL!'

KA-THOOM! KA-THOOM! KA-THOOM!

Elephant pulled—feet stomping, neck straining, trunk swinging up and down.

KER-SPLASH! KER-SPLASH! KER-SPLASH!

Crocodile pulled as well—feet splashing, teeth gnashing, tail thrashing back and forth.

They pulled for an hour. They pulled for two. But, pull as they might, neither could budge the other. At last, Elephant called through his aching teeth, 'Sparrow, I give up! I never would have believed it, but you are every bit as strong as I am. From now on I will tiptoe quietly past your tree.'

Crocodile called out, as well. 'You win, mighty Sparrow. From now on, you may drink from my river whenever you like.'

So Sparrow went home to her little nest. And when she told her babies what she had done, they laughed and clapped their wings and cheered, 'Too-tweet! Too-tweet! Too-tweet!' For their mother was now the strongest animal in the jungle!

Simple John

Once upon a time, there were three brothers who went off to seek their fortune.

The two older brothers were very clever. But the third brother was not clever at all. His name was John, and the two older brothers were not very nice to him. They made fun of him, and picked on him, and called him names like 'simple' and 'stupid' and 'fool'.

On the first day, they came across a huge mound of earth, tall and thin and teeming with ants.

'Ants are nasty!' shuddered the eldest brother.

'And they're good for nothing but treading on,' said the second brother.

But just as the two older brothers went to knock the anthill down, the third brother, John, stepped in their way.

'No!' he shouted. 'Ants are nice. They are black and tiny and creepy and crawly. And they're fun to watch. It wouldn't be kind to knock their house down.'

The older brothers looked at each other and shook their heads.

'Not very clever,' one whispered.

'Doesn't know a thing about insects,' whispered the other one.

But in the end they grew tired of arguing and agreed to leave the ants alone.

The next day, the three brothers came across a pond full of ducks.

'Ducks are tasty!' said the oldest brother.

'Ducks are delicious!' drooled the second brother.

But, just as the clever brothers aimed their arrows at the ducks, the third brother, John, stepped in their way.

'No!' he shouted. 'Ducks are nice. They have flappy wings and webby feet and quacky voices. It wouldn't be kind to kill them.'

The older brothers looked in the air and sighed.

'Doesn't know a thing about ducks,' one whispered.

'Nor good eating, neither,' whispered the other one.

But in the end they grew tired of arguing and agreed to leave the ducks alone.

On the third day, the three brothers came across a bees' nest tucked in the trunk of a thick, tall tree.

'Look at the honey!' said the oldest brother.

'Now that's good eating!' said the second brother.

But, just as the clever brothers were about to light a fire and smoke the bees out of the tree, the third brother, John, stepped in their way.

'No!' he shouted. 'Bees are nice. They are yellow and stripy and sticky and buzzy. It wouldn't be kind to steal their honey.'

The clever brothers crossed their arms and scowled.

'He's starting to get on my nerves,' whispered one.

'Mine, too,' whispered the other one.

But in the end they grew tired of arguing and agreed to leave the bees alone.

Later that day, the three brothers came to a castle. A castle with stone walls and stone towers and, standing inside, stone statue horses and peasants and princes. Indeed, the only thing that was not stone was a little bearded man who came to greet them.

'Thank you for coming,' he said. 'Thank you very much! We shall have some supper and get a good night's rest. Then tomorrow you must try to break the spell that has turned this castle to stone—and win for yourselves a great fortune!'

The brothers didn't know about breaking spells, but they were hungry and tired, and so they accepted the little man's invitation. They ate like horses and slept like logs. And, in the morning, it was the eldest brother who chose to go first.

'To break the spell,' explained the little man, 'you must perform three tasks. Before she was turned to stone, our Queen broke a necklace in the forest, and a thousand pearls were scattered across the ground. The first task is to gather up those pearls before sunset—or you, too, will be turned to stone.'

The eldest brother went out into the forest

to look for the pearls. They were everywhere! Under rocks and ferns and fallen leaves. But, clever as he was, he only managed to collect a hundred before the sun set. So he was turned to stone.

The next day, the second brother went to the forest. And, even though he managed to collect two hundred pearls, at the setting of the sun he too was turned to stone.

'What chance do I have?' thought John, as he set off on the third day. 'I'm not clever at all!' And then he heard a sound in the grass below.

'Hello, John!' called a tiny voice. 'I am the King of the Ants. You saved our anthill, and now we would like to help you. All my people are here—thousands of them!—and we will find the pearls for you.'

And so they did—every last one!

'Excellent!' said the little man. 'For your second task, you must find a silver key, which the Queen dropped in the lake.'

Again, poor John didn't know what to do. But just then, a big, brown duck flew over-head. 'Don't worry, John,' the duck called. 'You helped us and now we will help you.'

And with that, a whole flight of ducks plunged beneath the water, and came up again with the silver key.

'One more task,' the little man said, excited now. 'But we must hurry, for the sun is setting fast. The King has three daughters, who all look alike. But the one he loves the most was eating a little honey cake just before she was turned to stone. You must find her and kiss her.'

'No problem at all,' buzzed a voice in John's ear. 'I am the Queen Bee. And because you would not steal from us, I will help you find the princess.' The Queen Bee sniffed and sniffed at the lips of every stone girl in the castle, and finally she found one that smelled of honey.

John pursed his lips and kissed the stone statue, and immediately everything that had been turned to stone—including his brothers—became flesh and blood again!

And what was John's reward? He married the girl that he kissed. And his brothers married her sisters. And that is how the three brothers found their fortune—with the help of the least clever brother of them all.

The Selfish Sand Frog

Sand Frog was thirsty. So he went to the water-hole to have a drink. He drank and he drank and he drank. And the more he drank, the bigger he grew. He drank so much, in fact, that he drank that water-hole dry!

Dingo, Goanna, and Kangaroo complained. 'Hey, Sand Frog,' they cried, 'don't be so greedy. We need water, too!'

But Sand Frog ignored them. He was still thirsty, you see. So he hopped away to find more water.

Soon he came to a billabong. He drank and he drank and he drank. And the more he drank, the bigger he grew. He drank so much, in fact, that he drank that little swamp dry!

The newts and the tortoises and the tadpoles complained. 'Hey, Sand Frog,' they cried, 'don't be so greedy. We need water, too!'

But Sand Frog ignored them. He was still thirsty, you see. So he hopped away to find more water.

Soon he came to a lake. And you can guess what happened. He drank and he drank and he drank. And the more he drank, the bigger he grew. He drank so much, in fact, that he drank that lake dry!

The fish flipped and flopped around on the pebbly bottom. 'Hey, Sand Frog,' they complained, 'don't be so greedy. We need water, too!'

But Sand Frog ignored them. He was still thirsty, you see. So he hopped away to find more water.

Rivers and lakes and streams.

Swamps and ponds and creeks.

Sand Frog drank the water from them all—until there was no water left anywhere! And, by that time, he was so enormous that the only place he could find to sit was on the top of a great mountain.

The other animals were angry. So they grabbed their spears and set off to find him. Eagle saw him first, and he led the others to the mountain where Sand Frog sat.

'Give us our water back!' the animals cried. But, once again, Sand Frog ignored them. He wasn't thirsty any more. He was full. He was happy. And he was bigger than any of them.

One by one, the animals threw their sharp spears at Sand Frog.

Koala and Dingo and Bandicoot.

Platypus, Emu and Bat.

But each of them missed. Finally, Kangaroo aimed his long spear and threw it. He struck Sand Frog in the side, and the water gushed out of him, down the mountain, and back into the rivers and lakes and streams!

The other animals cheered. They drank and swam and splashed about.

But Sand Frog hopped sadly and painfully home. He was little again, and ashamed for having been so greedy. In fact, he dared not show his face to the other animals.

And that is why, even now, sand frogs hide in the sand all day, and only come out to play in the ponds at night.

The Mouse's Bride

It was an unusual family. An old man. An old woman. And a little mouse boy.

He was their dream-come-true. The old man and the old woman had no children of their own, but one day a hawk, soaring overhead, dropped the little mouse into the old woman's laundry basket. And from that moment on, the old man and she had raised him as their son.

The little mouse grew— as children do. And soon he was no longer a little mouse boy, but a full-grown mouse man. And he wanted more than anything to find a wife.

'I will help you, my son,' said the old man. So, one warm night they set off to find the mouse a bride. The old woman waved them goodbye and wiped the tears from her eyes, for she feared that she might never see her son again.

They walked and they walked and they walked, their path lit brightly by the light of the full moon. The moon watched, and grew curious, and at last she asked, 'What are you looking for?'

'A wife for my son,' the old man explained.

'I see,' said the moon. 'Well, I would make a very good wife. I am bright and beautiful and round! Would your son agree to marry me?'

The mouse looked at the moon and shook his little head.

'I'm sorry,' he said. 'You are indeed bright and beautiful and round. But you are also cold and distant. No, you are not the wife for me.'

So they walked and they walked and they walked some more, under the shadow of a dark night cloud. The cloud watched, and grew curious, and at last she asked, 'What are you looking for?'

'A wife for my son,' the old man explained.

'Ah,' said the cloud. 'Well, I would make an excellent wife. I am fluffy and puffy and soft!'

'Yes,' agreed the little mouse. 'But I have watched you, and you can also be angry and gloomy and very bad-tempered. No', he said, shaking his head again, 'you are not the wife for me.'

On they walked, far into the night now, and the wind whistled around them, and watched, and grew curious, and asked at last, 'What are you looking for?'

'A wife for my son,' said the old man again.

'Then look no further,' said the wind. 'For I would make the perfect wife. I can be both gentle and strong.'

'That is just the problem,' said the little mouse. 'You are one way and then another, and no one can tell which way it will be. No, you are not the wife for me.'

The old man and the mouse carried on a little further and, just as the old man was wondering if his son would ever find a wife, they came to a mountain.

'Ah!' said the mouse when he saw the mountain. 'Now there is the wife for me. She is tall and proud and full of life. And I can trust her to stand strong and true, whatever happens. Mountain,' he asked humbly, 'would you be my wife?'

'It would be a pleasure,' said the mountain. 'Now tunnel deep within me and you will find my heart.' The mouse began to dig. The old man helped him. And soon they came to a tunnel. And the tunnel led to a cave. And sitting in the middle of the cave was the most beautiful lady mouse that the little mouse had ever seen.

Together they went back to the old woman, who wept for joy when she saw them. Then the little mouse and the lady mouse were married. And they all lived happily ever after.

The Big Wave

The sea splashed gently against the sandy beach. The sandy beach lay white and hot before the little village. And in the little village lived four hundred people—old men and young men, mothers and grandmothers, babies and boys and girls.

Behind the village, green terraces rose like steps to a high, flat plateau. And on the plateau stood a fine old house, surrounded by rice fields.

In that house lived Hamaguchi—an old man, a rich man, owner of the rice fields and lord of the village below. With him lived his grandson—only ten years old, full of questions, and full of life.

One hot summer evening, Hamaguchi walked slowly out onto his porch. He looked at the village below, and smiled. It was harvest time, and his people were celebrating with music and dancing and bright lantern lights.

He looked at the beach beyond, cool and quiet and calm, and he smiled again.

But when Hamaguchi looked out across the sea, his smile turned suddenly to a worried frown. For there was a wave, a wave that stretched as far as he could see, tall and wild and fierce. And it was rushing towards the village below.

Hamaguchi had never seen this kind of wave. But he had heard tales about such waves from his father and his father's father. So he called his grandson and asked him to bring a flaming torch.

'Why, Grandfather?' the boy asked, innocently. 'Why do you want a torch?'

'There is no time to explain.' Hamaguchi answered. 'We must act quickly!' And he hobbled to the fields on the left of the house and set his crops on fire.

'Grandfather!' the boy cried. 'What are you doing?'

Hamaguchi looked down at the village. No one was looking up at the plateau.

'There is no time!' he barked. 'Come with me.' And he took the boy by the hand and set fire to the fields on the right.

The flames burst orange and yellow and white against the night, and the boy began to weep.

'Grandfather, are you mad? This is every-thing you own!'

But the old man said nothing. He looked down at the village, then hurried to the remaining fields and set the torch to them, as well. The sky was filled with sparks and smoke and the little boy was sobbing now.

'Please, Grandfather! Stop, Grandfather! There will be nothing left!'

Just then, a bell sounded, ringing from the temple in the village below. And soon, streaming up the terraced hill, came the villagers—young women, old women, boys and girls, fathers and grandfathers, babies on their backs and buckets in their hands. All four hundred of them—running to help put out the fire!

And, just as they reached the burning fields, the wave struck the village below.

It sounded like thunder.

It sounded like cannon fire.

It sounded like the hoof-beats of ten thousand horses.

It destroyed everything in its path, and when at last it rumbled and rolled back out to sea, there was not a single house left standing.

The people looked in horror at the ruins of their village. But when at last they turned to face the fields, they were gone as well—burned to the ground.

Hamaguchi's grandson grabbed him round the waist and, sobbing still, asked the question everyone else wanted to hear.

'Why, Grandfather? Why did you burn down your precious fields?'

'Don't you see?' the old man said to the crowd. 'I had to find some way to warn you—to lead you out of harm's way. For, as precious as my fields are to me, each and every one of you is more precious still.'

And with that, Hamaguchi invited them all to stay in his house until the village was rebuilt.

The old man lived many more years, but when, at last, he died, the people built a little shrine in their village, in memory of the lord who sacrificed all he had to save them from the terrible wave.

61

Tiger and the Storm

One evening, just as it was turning dark, Rabbit wandered out into the jungle, together with his wife and their friends, Owl and Dog.

Along the way, they spotted some fallen vines. So they stopped and gathered up the vines, hoping to weave them into a length of good, strong rope.

Suddenly, Rabbit heard something: the twitch of a tail, a long, low growl, the crush of a strong, striped paw.

'Tiger is coming,' he whispered to the others. 'Quick, hide behind that rock. And I will deal with him.'

The others did as Rabbit said and, just a moment later, Tiger burst out of the bushes.

'Aha!' he roared. 'I have you cornered once again. There is no way you can escape this time!'

'Oh dear,' said Rabbit sadly. 'You have such bad timing, Tiger. Haven't you heard? There is a great storm coming this way—a hurricane, I believe—and I was just tying myself to this tree so I would not be blown away. If you have any sense, I suggest you do the same.'

'Nonsense!' Tiger roared. 'This is just another one of your tricks. You have made a fool of me before, but I will not be fooled again!'

'All right,' Rabbit sighed. 'Eat me if you like. But before you have finished, the storm will blow you clear across the jungle. Listen,' (and he said this in the direction of the rock) 'you can hear the pitter-patter of rain even now.'

Rabbit's wife was listening. So she began to thump the ground with her big back legs: pitter-patter, pitter-patter, pitter-patter.

'Oh dear,' Tiger paused. 'Perhaps you are right, after all. But perhaps it is nothing more than a light shower! I will eat you now. I don't mind getting wet.'

'A light shower?' Rabbit said quickly. 'Then how is it that I hear the wind blowing up into a storm?'

It was Owl's turn this time. He started to flap his big brown wings, and he called, 'Hoo-hoo. Hoo-hoo. Hoo-hoo.'

'Oh my!' Tiger was shaking now. 'I believe a storm is coming, after all. But I am sure I still have time to eat you!'

'Perhaps,' nodded Rabbit, 'But then who will be left to help tie you to this tree? Listen, the wind is howling even harder now. The storm is almost here!'

And now Dog joined in, howling, 'A-Woo! A-Woo! A-Woo!'

'All right, then. All right,' Tiger whimpered.

'Quickly, tie me to the tree. And tie me tight!'

So Rabbit did just as Tiger asked. He wrapped the vines around Tiger's striped legs and Tiger's striped belly and he tied him to the tree. And all the while, his friends kept up their thumping and their hooting and their howling.

'There you go,' announced Rabbit, once Tiger was tied tightly to the tree. 'That should keep you from going anywhere for a while.'

'But what about you?' Tiger asked.

'Oh, don't worry about me.' Rabbit chuckled. 'I feel very safe, now. I think the storm has passed us by. Listen.'

And suddenly, the thumping and the hooting and the howling came to an end. And Rabbit's friends came out, chuckling, from behind the rock.

'You've done it again!' Tiger roared. 'You've tricked me. And you're in trouble, now!'

But when Tiger went to leap at Rabbit, he found that he could not move. No, not one inch—so tightly had Rabbit tied him to that tree!

'Let me go! Let me go—NOW!' Tiger roared.

But Rabbit just grinned.

'I don't think so,' he said. 'For if there is one thing more dangerous than a howling storm, it's an angry, howling Tiger!'

And with that, he and his friends disappeared into the night—safe once more.

The Knee-High Man

Knee-High Man lived by a swamp, deep in the heart of Alabama.

He lived by himself, in a tiny, run-down shack, because he was ashamed of how small he was.

'I'm tired of being little,' he said to himself, one day. 'I'm gonna find out how to get big!'

So he went to the biggest friend he knew. He went to see Mr Horse.

'Mr Horse!' he hollered. 'Mr Horse, I want to be big, like you. Tell me what I have to do.'

Mr Horse munched thoughtfully on a mouthful of oats.

'Well…' he said slowly. 'I always eat lots and lots of oats. Then I run and run—about twenty miles a day. That's how I got big. Maybe that'll work for you.'

'Thank you,' said Knee-High Man. Then he did just what Mr Horse said.

He ate oats till his stomach hurt.

He ran and ran till his little legs hurt.

But still he grew no bigger. No, not one little bit.

So he went to see his next-biggest friend. He went to see Mr Bull.

'Mr Bull!' he hollered. 'Mr Bull, I want to be big, like you. Tell me what I have to do.'

Mr Bull munched patiently on a mouthful of grass.

'Well…' he grunted. 'I chew up field after field of grass. Then I bellow and bellow— MOOO!—for all I'm worth. That's how I got big. Maybe that'll work for you.'

'Thank you,' said Knee-High Man. Then he did just what Mr Bull said.

He chewed grass till his teeth hurt.

He bellowed—MOOO!—till his throat hurt.

But still he grew no bigger. No, not one little bit.

So he went to see the smartest friend he knew. He went to see Mr Hoot Owl.

'Mr Hoot Owl!' he hollered. 'Mr Hoot Owl, I'm tired of being a little Knee-High Man. I want to be big! Please tell me what I have to do.'

Mr Hoot Owl blinked and ruffled his feathers and turned his big head round and round.

'Hoo-hoo! Tell me, Mr Knee-High Man,' he said, at last. 'Why do you want to be big?'

'Because I'm tired of always looking up at everyone,' moaned Knee-High Man.

Mr Hoot Owl blinked and ruffled his feathers again.

'Hoo-hoo! Size isn't everything,' he said. 'Can you climb a tree?'

'Of course!' answered Knee-High Man.

'Then come on up here and join me,' said the owl.

Knee-High Man climbed up that tree, as fast as any squirrel. Then he sat himself down on the branch beside Mr Hoot Owl.

'Now look around,' said Mr Hoot Owl. 'What do you see?'

Knee-High Man looked. There was Mr Horse, running around his field. And over there was Mr Bull, bellowing for all he was worth. And neither of them looked any bigger than the biggest ant!

'When you get tired of being small,' said Mr Hoot Owl, just climb up here. You'll be the tallest thing around! And when you get tired of that, climb back down—and be satisfied with what you are.'

So that's just what he did.

And he was never ashamed of being a Knee-High Man again.

The Clever Baker

Annie was a baker—the best in all Scotland. Shortbreads and buns and cakes—she made them all. And they were so delicious that no one ever left a crumb behind, on table or plate or floor.

Now this was fine for everyone but the fairies, who depended on those crumbs, and who had never had so much as a tiny taste of one of Annie's famous cakes. So one bright morning, the Fairy King decided to do something about that. He hid himself among the wild flowers by the side of the road, and when Annie passed on her way to market, he sprinkled fairy dust in her eyes to make her fall fast asleep.

When Annie awoke, she was no longer on the road, but deep in fairyland, face to face with the Fairy King.

'Annie!' the King commanded. 'Everyone has tasted your wonderful cakes. Everyone, but us! So from now on, you will stay here in fairyland and bake for us every day.'

'Oh dear,' thought Annie. But she didn't show that she was worried, or even scared, for she was a clever woman. No, she set her mind, at once, to making a plan for her escape.

'Very well,' she said. 'But if I am to bake you a cake, I will need ingredients—flour and milk, eggs and sugar and butter.'

'Fetch them at once!' commanded the Fairy King. So off the fairies flew, to Annie's house. And back they flew, in a flash, with everything she needed.

'Oh dear,' Annie sighed, shaking her head (and still without a plan). 'If I am to bake a cake, I will also need my tools—my pots and pans and pitchers and bowls and spoons.'

'Fetch them, quickly!' the Fairy King commanded again. But when the fairies returned, they were in such a hurry that they stumbled and sent the pots and pans crashing and clanking across the floor.

'OOH! OWW!' cried the Fairy King, jamming his hands against his ears. 'You know very well that I cannot stand loud noises!'

And, at that moment, Annie had her plan.

She broke the eggs and poured the milk and mixed in the flour and butter. But when she stirred the batter, she made the spoon clatter—clackety, clackety, clack—against the side of the bowl.

The Fairy King winced at the noise, but Annie could see that it was not loud enough.

And so she said, 'Oh dear. I am used to having my little yellow cat beside me when I bake. I cannot make my best cake unless he is here.'

So the Fairy King commanded, and the fairies went, and came back at once with the cat.

Annie put the cat under the table and, as she mixed the batter, she trod, ever so gently, on the cat's tail.

And so the spoon went, 'Clackety, clackety, clack!'

And the cat went, 'Yow! Yow! Yow!'

And the Fairy King looked even more uncomfortable.

'Oh dear,' said Annie again. 'It's still not right. I'm also used to having my big brown dog beside me when I bake. I don't suppose…?'

'Yes, yes,' sighed the Fairy King. 'Anything for a taste of that cake.'

And the fairies were sent for the dog.

Annie put him next to the cat, and he soon began to bark.

And so the spoon went, 'Clackety, clackety, clack!'

And the cat went, 'Yow! Yow! Yow!'

And the dog went, 'Woof! Woof! Woof!'

And the Fairy King stuck a fairy finger in one ear.

'Just one more thing,' said Annie. 'I am worried about my little baby. And I cannot do my best work when I am worried.'

'All right, all right,' moaned the Fairy King.

And he sent off his fairies one more time.

The baby was asleep when she arrived, but as soon as she heard all the noise, she awoke with a cry.

And so the spoon went, 'Clackety, clackety, clack!'

And the cat went, 'Yow! Yow! Yow!'

And the dog went, 'Woof! Woof! Woof!'

And the baby went, 'Wah! Wah! Wah!'

And the Fairy King put his hands over his ears and shouted, 'Enough! Enough! Enough!'

And everything went quiet.

'Even the best cake in the world is not worth this racket,' he cried. 'Take your baby, woman, and your dog and your cat and your noisy spoon. Go back to your own world, and leave us in peace!'

Annie smiled. 'I'll do better than that,' she said. 'If you promise to leave me be, I'll put a special little cake for you and your people by the fairy mound each day.'

'That's a bargain,' smiled the Fairy King, and Annie and all that belonged to her were returned to her kitchen in a flash.

And every day, from then on, Annie left a little cake by the fairy mound. And the Fairy King not only left her alone; each day he left her a little bag of gold, where the cake had been. And they all lived happily ever after.

How the Kangaroo Got Its Tail

There was a time when Kangaroo had no tail. Not a bushy tail. Not a waggly tail. And certainly not the long, strong tail he has today.

Kangaroo had no tail. But what he did have were plenty of children. So many children, in fact, that some of the other animals were jealous—particularly Bandicoot, who had no children at all.

One day, Bandicoot came to visit Kangaroo.

'Kangaroo,' he pleaded. 'You and your wife have six beautiful children, and I have none at all. Won't you give me three of your children to raise as my own?'

Kangaroo was shocked. 'No,' he said, as politely as he could. 'We love our children. We could never give them away.'

'Two, then,' begged Bandicoot. 'Just let me have two. I promise to be a good father.'

'No,' Kangaroo insisted. 'We want to raise our children ourselves, thank you very much.'

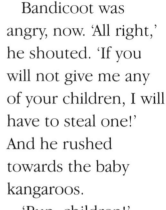

'How about one, then,' Bandicoot cried. 'Just one, and I will never bother you again.'

'No!' said Kangaroo, firmly. 'We could not part with even one of our children!'

Bandicoot was angry, now. 'All right,' he shouted. 'If you will not give me any of your children, I will have to steal one!' And he rushed towards the baby kangaroos.

'Run, children!' Kangaroo hollered. 'Run away!'

The kangaroo children jumped from their mother's pouch and turned to run, but Bandicoot was too quick for them. He grabbed one of the little kangaroos from behind and held on tight.

Kangaroo was there in a second. He grabbed his child by the arms, and both he and Bandicoot began to pull.

They pulled and they pulled and they pulled. And then something strange happened.

The little kangaroo's bottom began to stretch—it grew longer and longer and longer!

'Help me, wife!' Kangaroo called. So she began to pull as well. And the little kangaroo's bottom stretched longer still.

Finally, Kangaroo called for his other children, and when they began to pull, it was too much for Bandicoot. He let go with a sigh and ran away. And the kangaroos tumbled down in a pile of pouches and feet and fur.

'Is everyone all right?' asked Kangaroo.

'Yes,' said Mother Kangaroo.

'Yes,' said five little kangaroos.

But the last little kangaroo cried, 'Look!' And he waved his new, long tail.

His brothers and sisters began to laugh, but when they saw how much better he could run and jump, they soon wanted long tails too.

And from that time to this very day, there has never been a kangaroo without one!

The Greedy Farmer

It was nearly dark by the time poor Farmer Idris finished milking his cows. He yawned and he stretched and he made his way slowly from his ramshackle barn to his tumbledown house. Another day of hard work done—and very little to show for it.

But at the side of the cool, green lake that bordered Farmer Idris' land, another farmer's work had just begun. The sun had barely dropped behind the hills when the Fairy of the Lake walked slowly out of the water.

She was beautiful and tall, and dressed in a dripping, lake-green gown. She sang a song— the sound bubbling out of her, cool and clear as a mountain spring. And in response to that sound, a herd of pure milk-white cows came up out of the water after her and grazed on the grass at the side of the lake.

When dawn arrived, and the sun peeped its head over the hills, she returned to the water, her cows following behind. All but one, that is, who had wandered off towards Farmer Idris' house. All that day she grazed with his cows and later that evening followed them back to his barn.

Farmer Idris was surprised to see a milk-white cow among his herd. But as she had no markings and appeared to belong to no one, he kept her and milked her with the rest.

And from that moment on, the surprises never stopped! She gave more milk in one day than his whole herd could give in a week. And the taste of it—Oh! It was richer and purer than any milk he had ever drunk. There was soft, sweet butter, as well, and smooth, golden cheese, and thick, heavy cream. And people would come from miles around to smell it, to taste it, and to buy it.

After many months, the milk-white cow gave birth to calves, and when they had grown, their milk was just as good as hers.

And so the years passed, the herd grew, and poor Farmer Idris became rich Farmer Idris. And then, sadly, greedy Farmer Idris.

'The milk-white cow is growing old,' he complained to his wife, one day. 'Soon she will be no good for milking. I say we fatten her up and see how much money we can get from the butcher.'

'But she has been such a good cow,' his wife answered. 'Why not let her wander the fields and graze her days away?'

'A waste of good grass!' Farmer Idris huffed. 'No, we shall fatten her up. She'll fetch good money—you'll see.'

So that's what Farmer Idris did. He fattened her up till she was bigger than any cow ever seen in those parts. Then he carted her off to the butcher's—the townspeople oohing and aahing at the size and sight of her.

The butcher held her milk-white head steady. He raised his axe above her. But, just as he was about to let it fall, he heard a song echo through the valley where the little town lay. The crowd looked to the hills round about them, and there was the Fairy of the Lake standing on the highest crag, beautiful and tall in her lake-green gown.

'Follow me, milk-white cow,' she sang. 'Come away, milk-white cow. Come with me to your home in the deep-green lake.'

Off ran the milk-white cow, galloping after the Fairy—up the hill and across the fields and towards the lake. And not only the cow, but her children and grandchildren as well— every milk-white cow in Farmer Idris' herd!

Farmer Idris ran after the cows, ran as fast as he could. And he caught up with them, just as they were walking into the lake— milk-white lilies blooming at the spot where each cow disappeared beneath the water.

He called for them. He begged them to return. He promised that the milk-white cow could graze happily on his fields for ever. But there was no answer. And soon, without his herd of fairy cows, the greedy farmer became poor Farmer Idris all over again.

The Generous Bird

Once upon a time there was a bird. Not a bright and beautiful kind of bird that soared across the sky. Nor a sleek and graceful kind of bird that sailed across the water. But a plain and ordinary kind of bird that stretched out its scrawny neck and pecked at the ground as it scratched along.

And as for its song—well, this bird had no song at all. No chirp. No screech. No hoot. Nothing, not a peep!

'Tell me,' said the bird to the sun, one day. 'What am I good for? I am not beautiful. I am not graceful. I can't even sing.'

'Ah,' the sun beamed back. 'There is much that you are good for. You have a gift, a special gift, that belongs to no other bird. And if you look, I am sure that you will find it.'

And so, the very next day, the bird set off across the wide world—knees jerking, head bobbing, droopy tail dragging behind—to find what he was good for.

At the end of the first day, he came to a village. Most of the people had gone in for the night, but there was someone still out in the street—a little, brown-haired girl who sobbed and sniffed and called out in a mournful voice, 'Here Collie! Come back, Collie! Where are you, Collie?'

'What's the matter?' the bird asked the little girl.

'It's my dog,' she sobbed and sniffed again. 'He's run away, and I can't find him.'

'Oh dear,' said the bird, sadly. 'If I were like other birds, I could soar up into the sky and look for him. But I'm not very good at flying, you see.'

The little girl sobbed and sniffed once more. And then cried so hard that the bird thought his heart would break.

'I'll tell you what,' he said. 'Why don't I walk with you, and keep you company while you look for him?'

So they walked together through the night.

And the little girl called out, 'Collie, Collie! Come back Collie!' in her sad and mournful voice.

But Collie did not come, so they lay down, at last, behind an old fence, and the little girl grabbed the bird tight and held him for comfort the whole night long.

When the sun stuck his head over the rooftops and announced the return of morning, the little girl rubbed her eyes and then opened them. And there, standing before her, was Collie! She leaped up and hugged her dog, and then turned to thank the bird.

'I didn't do anything.' he said.

'Yes you did,' the little girl smiled. 'You stayed with me, and you helped me feel better.'

The bird left the little girl and her dog and walked for another day, knees jerking, head bobbing, droopy tail dragging behind. And he came, at last, to a town.

Everyone was asleep. Everyone, that is, but an old woman who sat alone on the ground.

'What are you staring at?' she growled at the bird.

'Nothing,' he said. 'You look so unhappy, that's all. If I was like other birds, I could sing you a pretty song and cheer you up.'

'I don't need anybody cheering me up!' she snarled. 'I don't need anybody at all!' And

then she started to cry. 'Who am I fooling?' she wept. 'I'm all alone because I've been awful to people all my life. To my husband. To my children. To my friends.' And before she could finish, the sky opened up and answered her tears with tears of its own.

'You're getting all wet,' said the bird. 'You'll catch cold!' So he hopped up onto a nearby wall and draped his droopy tail over her head and shoulders. And that's how he spent the night, with the rain dripping down his droopy tail and the sad old woman huddled underneath.

The rain had stopped by the time the sun blinked the new day awake.

'Thank you,' said the woman to the bird. And she even managed a little smile. 'It's nice to know I have at least one friend in this world.'

The bird set off once again, knees jerking, head bobbing, soggy tail dragging and drooping behind.

It was dark by the time he arrived at the city. But there was still plenty of noise in the city streets. So he crept into an alley to find a quiet place to sleep. But just as he was nestling down, a little boy came tearing round the corner. He was puffing and panting, and a shaft of moonlight showed his face bruised, purple and black and blue.

'What's the matter?' said the bird.

'They're after me,' panted the boy. 'Bullies. They've already beaten me up once and they want to do it again!'

'Oh dear,' sighed the bird. 'If I was like other birds, I could pick you up in my strong claws and carry you safely away. But I'm not like other birds, am I? So here's what we'll do...'

The bird hurried the boy into the darkest corner. Then he spread his wings and tail as wide as he could and wrapped them around the boy, so the bullies saw nothing but a dark lump when they rushed into the alley.

'There he is!' they shouted, and they showered the bird with bricks and rocks and stones. But when they took a closer look, one of them said, 'Hey, it's not him. It's nothing but an ugly, dead bird.'

The bird wasn't dead, but when the sun finally yawned his morning 'hello', he was very bruised and sore. The little boy huddled beneath him, however, was safe and warm.

The boy went to say 'thank you', but when he saw the bird, all he could do was point and say, 'Look! You're different!'

And so he was. His back and tail were streaked purple and black and blue, and covered with delicate raindrop patterns. And when he opened his mouth to speak, out came a haunting 'Col-Col-Collie' song!

Don't you see?' beamed the sun. 'Your gift was the kindness that springs from a loving heart. And now the marks of your love will be with you always—for all the world to see.'

And that is how the peacock came to be the most beautiful of all the birds!

Tiger Eats a Monkey

Tiger sat silently in the shade of the tamarind tree. He was waiting. Waiting for some careless creature to wander within reach of his terrible claws.

Rabbit stood still at the top of the tamarind tree. He was watching. Watching for Tiger, of course. But he hadn't a clue that his enemy was hiding below.

Suddenly, a jumble of monkeys came tumbling across the jungle floor, breaking the silence with their hooting and scratching and screeching.

78

They tumbled past the tamarind tree, one by one, but the last monkey, the littlest of them all, tumbled too close to Tiger.

'Got you!' Tiger growled, as he grabbed the monkey by the tail and went to gobble him up.

'Wait just a minute!' called Rabbit from the treetop. 'What do you think you're doing?'

'Eating a monkey,' said Tiger, matter-of-factly. 'What business is it of yours?'

'None at all,' shrugged Rabbit. 'As long as you don't mind looking stupid.'

'Stupid?' said Tiger, puzzled. 'How?'

'It's obvious, isn't it?' sighed Rabbit. 'You're eating that monkey all wrong!'

Tiger looked at the monkey. The monkey looked at Tiger. They were both puzzled.

'Listen,' Rabbit continued. 'It's very simple. Monkeys are not meant to be shoved in the mouth and swallowed in one bite. No! Monkeys are meant to be enjoyed, bit by monkey bit. That's why you always toss a monkey in the air and catch him with your teeth—like a nut or a piece of fruit. Everybody knows that.'

'Everybody?' said the Tiger, looking again at the monkey.

'Everybody,' the monkey stammered, nodding his head and hoping that Rabbit knew what he was doing.

'Well, I don't want to look stupid,' Tiger said, at last. 'So, here goes!' And he tossed the little monkey high into the air.

'Now open your mouth and shut your eyes,' called Rabbit. 'This is going to taste GRRREAT!' Quickly, he grabbed the monkey and pulled him to safety, and dropped some bitter tamarind fruit in his place!

Tiger caught the fruit in his open mouth— it was a perfect catch! But instead of sweet monkey meat, his mouth was filled with the strongest, nastiest stuff he had ever tasted.

Tiger spat and hissed and howled, but the taste would not go away.

So he raced off to the river to wash the awful taste out of his mouth. And when he had gone, Rabbit and the monkey climbed down from the tree.

The monkey's family screeched and hooted and cheered, and then tumbled away into the jungle. And Rabbit just smiled, happy that Tiger still hadn't learned how to eat a monkey!

Lazy Tom

Tom, the farmer's son, was lazy. Everybody knew it, and even he didn't mind admitting it. He knew he should have been tending to the cows, or helping out in the fields. But it was much nicer just strolling along the hedge-lined paths, chewing on a piece of straw, wasting the day away.

And then Tom heard something—a click-clacking kind of noise coming from the other side of the hedge. He thought it was a squirrel at first. Or a bird, maybe. But when it went on and on, at a strong and steady beat, he grew curious. So he crept quietly round the edge of the hedge and peeked.

It was not a squirrel. Nor any kind of bird. No, it was a tiny little man, with a leather apron hung round his neck, hammering together a wee pair of shoes.

'A leprechaun!' thought Tom. 'Here's my chance to find a fortune!'

Tom moved quietly towards the little fellow, not taking his eyes off him for a second. For Tom knew that to look away from a leprechaun was to give him the chance to escape. Closer and closer Tom crept. And, what with Tom fixing his eyes on the tiny man and the click-clacking of that hammer, the leprechaun did not move an inch until Tom grabbed him with both hands and hoisted him in the air.

'Gotcha!' Tom cried. And, struggle as he might, the leprechaun could not wriggle free.

'What is it you want, then?' the leprechaun sighed. 'And be quick about it. There's work to be done. Not that you'd know anything about that,' he added. 'For if I'm not mistaken, you're Lazy Tom, the farmer's son.'

'So I am!' Tom grinned. 'But soon I shall be Rich Tom—and I won't have to lift a finger to do it—for I want nothing more or nothing less than for you to take me to your famous pot of gold!'

The leprechaun sighed again. 'Then I shall show you where it is,' he said. 'Take my hand and follow me.'

Tom set the leprechaun down, grabbed his hand and followed him through pasture and

wood and stream. Finally, they came to a
field covered with bright blue flowers. The
leprechaun led Tom to a plant somewhere
near the middle, and then he stopped.

'Dig under here,' the leprechaun said.
'And you will find my pot of gold.'

'Dig?' cried Tom. 'You said nothing about
digging!'

'Well,' answered the leprechaun. 'I only
promised to show you where it was. And
I have done so. Now you must keep your
promise and let me go!'

81

'All right,' replied Tom. 'But you must promise me one more thing.' And he took his handkerchief out of his pocket and tied it round the top of the plant. 'I am going home to fetch a spade. You must promise to leave this handkerchief here until I return.'

The leprechaun looked at the handkerchief. The leprechaun looked at Tom. Then he grinned a little grin and nodded his little head.

'That I promise, as well,' he agreed. And then he disappeared.

Tom hurried back to his house, and after much asking (for he hadn't a clue where the tools were), he found a shovel. Then he hurried even more quickly back to the field. Through pasture and wood and stream he raced. He had never worked so hard in his life! But when, at last, he reached the field of bright blue flowers, he stopped his running, dropped his shovel, and stared.

The leprechaun had kept his promise. Tom's handkerchief was still tied to one of the blue flowers. But there were also handkerchiefs tied to all the other plants in that vast field—hundreds and hundreds of them, so that Tom had no idea which one belonged to him!

He could have dug them all up. But he was Lazy Tom, after all. So he shrugged his shoulders, and picked up his shovel. And, to the chirping of the birds and the chattering of the squirrels and the click-clacking of one sly little leprechaun shoemaker, he stumbled off towards home.

The Contented Priest

Once upon a time, there lived a fat and contented priest who served a skinny little king.

'I am much richer than you!' the king moaned to the priest, one day. 'Yet, look at me. I am nothing more than a sad bag of skin and bones. How is it that you came to be so happy and hearty and round?'

'It's very simple,' the priest chuckled. 'You worry over many things: collecting your taxes and waging your wars. It's the worry that makes you thin. As for me, I simply trust that God will take care of everything I need.'

'It's that simple, is it?' the king sneered. 'Then I shall give you something to worry about, and we'll see how happy and hearty you remain. In three days' time, you must return to my palace and give me the answers to the following three questions: What am I worth? Where is the middle of the earth? And what am I thinking? Answer correctly, and you shall have your weight in gold. Answer wrongly, and my dark dungeon will be your new home!'

The king smiled as a worried shadow fell across the fat priest's face.

'Now go!' the king commanded. And we shall see how happy you are when you return.'

All the way home, the priest worried over the king's three questions: How much is the king worth? Where is the middle of the earth? What is the king thinking? 'How can I possibly answer these questions?' the priest wondered.

83

His head hurt. His stomach churned. And he was wet with sweat. But right then and there, he decided to worry no longer.

'I will do what I always do,' he said to himself. 'I will pray, and trust God to take care of me.'

The priest prayed for one whole day. But no answers came.

He prayed for another day. And still no answers.

But on the third day, as he sat at his window with his head bowed, an answer came in a very strange way… There was a tapping on the glass. It was the priest's gardener.

'Excuse me, Father,' the gardener said. 'But I couldn't help noticing. For the last two days you have done nothing but kneel at this window. Is something wrong?'

The priest invited the gardener inside and described his most unusual problem.

The old gardener shook his head. 'Those are hard questions to be sure. But I think I can help you—if you will do one thing.'

'Anything!' the priest agreed.

'Lend me your priest's black robe.'

The priest scratched his bald head. 'But my robe is far too big for you,' he said. 'Why, you're even smaller and skinnier than the king himself!'

'Exactly!' the gardener grinned.

Later that day, the gardener knocked on the door of the palace. He was wrapped from top to bottom in the priest's bulky, black robe. And he wore a thick, black hood over his head.

The king was delighted when he saw him.

'Look at him!' the king said gleefully to one of his guards. 'Just three days of worry has made him even skinnier than me!'

But when he spoke to the man in the robe, his skinny face was grim.

'And now for the three questions,' he said sternly. 'Number One: How much am I worth?'

The gardener paused for a moment. And then, trying to sound as much like the priest as possible, he answered, 'Twenty-nine pieces of silver—and not one penny more.'

'Twenty-nine pieces of silver?' the king scoffed. 'I am worth far more than that! However did you come up with such a ridiculously small amount?'

'Well, Your Majesty,' the gardener replied. 'Everyone knows that the Lord Jesus was sold for thirty pieces of silver. Surely you do not claim to be worth more than him?'

Now it was the king's turn to pause. 'No… no… of course not,' he muttered. 'Well answered.'

Then he looked straight at the man in the robe. 'But what about the next question?' he continued. 'Where is the middle of the earth?'

The gardener tapped his foot on the palace floor. 'Right under here,' he said confidently. 'And I dare you to prove me wrong!'

The king was stuck. He could not prove where the middle of the earth was any more than the gardener could. So he moved on to the final question.

'Here is one you will never get!' the king chuckled. 'Tell me—what am I thinking?'

'Oh, that's easy!' the gardener chuckled back. 'You think that I am the priest!'

'Of course I do,' the king replied.

'Ah, but I am not!' said the gardener, throwing off the big, black robe. 'But you thought I was. And so I knew exactly what you were thinking!'

The king was surprised for a second.

And then angry for another.

But when he realized how clever this little gardener had been, he smiled, and then, for the first time in a long time, he laughed. And finally he called for his treasurer.

'This man deserves his weight in gold!' the king announced. 'And the priest deserves the same, for he has taught me a lesson about worry.'

So the priest was saved from the dungeon.

The gardener became a wealthy man.

The king tried to worry a little less often.

And they all lived happily ever after.

Olle and the Troll

Olle had never seen a troll. He was only five years old.

'Trolls are ugly!' said his mother. 'They have turnip noses and berry-bush eyebrows.'

'Trolls are scary!' said his father. 'Their mouths run right from ear to ear and their left hand is always a wolf's paw.'

'Trolls are dangerous!' said his parents

together. 'The Troll of the Big Mountain stuffed our best two goats in his big sack and carried them away. And if you are not careful, he will do the same to you!'

Olle had never seen a troll. But if he ever did see one, he knew exactly what he would do. He had a stick with a hard wood knot at the end. And two boards hammered together to make a sword.

'I'll chop him to bits!' Olle boasted to his parents. 'I'll take care of that Troll if he comes round here again.'

'You'll do no such thing!' his father warned him. 'If that Troll comes to the door, you'll keep it locked tight and call for me. And that Troll will leave you alone.'

Olle had never seen a troll. But the Troll of the Big Mountain had seen him. And he decided, one day, to stuff Olle in his sack and carry him away. So he waited for Olle's parents to start their day's work, then he tramped down the Big Mountain to Olle's house.

Along the way, he disguised himself. He pulled a hood over his ugly head and wrapped a bandage around his wolf-paw hand. He stooped and walked with a limp and looked for all the world like a withered old man.

The Troll banged on Olle's door, and Olle looked nervously out of the window. Olle had never seen a troll. And this visitor looked nothing like the horrible creature his parents had described.

'Who is it?' he called.

'Just an old man,' lied the Troll, in a feeble little voice. 'I've lost a coin on your step. My eyesight isn't what it used to be. Could you come and help me find it?'

'Oh no,' said Olle. 'My parents told me to stay inside, with the door locked. There is an evil, ugly troll about who likes to carry off little boys.'

'Do I look like an evil, ugly troll?' the Troll asked.

'Well… no,' Olle admitted. 'But if you were, I'd chop you in pieces with my stick and my sword. See!' And Olle held his little weapons to the window.

'It's hard to see from out here,' the Troll said. 'Perhaps if you were to let me come inside…'

Olle didn't know what to do. But the old man looked harmless enough. So he opened the door.

The Troll examined the weapons carefully, chuckling to himself and waiting for the right moment to grab the boy.

'The Troll stole our goats,' Olle explained. 'I didn't have my stick and sword then, but if I had…'

'Goats?' interrupted the Troll. 'Did you say goats? Why, just this morning, I saw a whole herd of goats, up on the Big Mountain.'

'But that's where the Troll lives!' Olle exclaimed.

'I could take you there,' said the Troll, slyly. 'We could bring your goats back!'

'Yes, please!' Olle said. 'My parents will be so surprised!'

'Indeed they will,' the Troll grinned. And off they went—but not before Olle had stuck his sword and stick in his belt and shoved a crusty chunk of bread into his pocket.

Olle had never seen a troll (even though there was now one walking beside him!). So, of course, he didn't know anything about troll secrets. He'd never have guessed that if a troll accepts a gift from someone, he can never do that someone any harm.

It was a long walk to the Big Mountain. And halfway there Olle got hungry. So he sat down on the grass, plucked the chunk of bread out of his pocket and tore off a piece. And, being a polite little boy, he offered a piece to the Troll.

'No. No, thank you,' said the Troll, firmly

(for he knew the troll secrets better than anyone). And, besides, the time had come to stuff Olle into his sack.

This, of course, had to be done in just the right way. There was no point, the Troll thought, in making off with a little boy if one could not see him struggle and scream and squirm!

And so the Troll grinned a wicked grin and said, 'Tell me, Olle, what would you do if I were not an old man at all, but that ugly, evil Troll?'

Olle looked at the Troll and smiled. 'That's silly,' he said. 'You're the nicest man I've ever met!'

Well, the Troll was so pleased with his evil joke, that he threw back his head, opened his ugly, wide mouth and roared with laughter.

And he would have laughed and laughed and laughed, if Olle had not seen this as the perfect opportunity to share what was left of his bread. He tossed a piece—a little round ball of a piece—right into the Troll's open mouth. And, though the Troll gagged and choked and coughed, in the end there was nothing he could do but swallow the bread. And that meant, of course, that he could no longer do Olle any harm!

In fact, he did just the opposite. He led Olle to the lost goats, and watched sadly as the little boy shepherded them down the hill and out of sight.

There was a great celebration when Olle and the goats returned home. His parents were surprised. Their friends were amazed. But Olle was just a little disappointed.

'I've been all the way to the Big Mountain and back,' he complained. 'And I *still* haven't seen a troll!'

The Steel Man

One by one, the steel-working men huffed and puffed and struggled to lift the long steel beams. It was a contest—a contest that took place once a year in the smoky shadow of the steel mill—to prove who was the strongest man in the steel-making valley.

But as the light of the setting sun mingled with the blast-furnace soot and fire, not a man among them had yet been able to lift the heaviest beam of all.

Suddenly they heard something—Boom! Boom! Boom! Then they felt the earth shake. And finally, they saw him, tramping through the twilight, hammering the ground with his

steel-tipped shoes—a giant of a man, nine feet tall at least, with hands like shovels and a head full of burnt brown hair!

He lumbered through the crowd, right up to the heaviest steel beam. Then he wrapped one hairy fist around it—and swung it up over his head!

The crowd gasped. They had never seen anyone so strong. But the big man just tilted back his head and laughed—a rumbling, tumbling sound, like steel makes as it bubbles and boils in the furnace.

'Let me introduce myself,' he roared. 'My father was the sun, hotter than any furnace. My mother was Mother Earth herself. And I was born in the belly of an ore-bearing mountain. For I am a man who is made of steel! And my name is Joe Magarac.'

Now it was the crowd's turn to laugh. For in their language, the word 'magarac' meant 'donkey'!

'Laugh all you want,' the big man chuckled. 'Because all I want to do is eat like a donkey and work like a donkey!'

The steel-working men laughed again, and clapped and cheered. Then they gathered round Joe and introduced themselves.

But high in the steel mill, in the fancy room where the bosses worked, there was another man—the Big Boss, the man who owned the steel mill. His face was pressed to the window

and, through the grime and the smoke, he could see what was going on in the yard below.

'He's a strong man.' The Big Boss smiled. 'So I will hire him to work for me. Then maybe I won't need to hire so many other men.'

Joe started every day in the same way. He gobbled up a bucket of coal, and washed it down with a bowl of steaming, hot steel soup. Then he tramped over to the mill, picking his teeth with a hard, cold chisel.

He grabbed a pile of old railroad tracks with one arm, and ten tons of iron ore with the other. Then he carried them over to Furnace Number Nine and dumped them in. And finally he shovelled coal underneath and set the whole thing burning with a finger-snap spark.

The stuff inside the furnace started to melt. It turned red and orange and yellow and white hot. But that heat didn't bother Joe. No, he stuck his arm in there and stirred it around. 'Kind of tickles,' he laughed.

And then, as that stuff cooled down, thick and gooey, Joe grabbed a handful in his fist and squeezed it tight. And out between his fingers oozed four perfect steel beams!

Day by day, week by week, month by month, those beams piled up. Until the warehouses were full. And the steel yard. And, at last, the mill itself.

And that's when the Big Boss came down from his fancy room.

'Boys!' he hollered. 'I got some bad news for you. Joe Magarac, here, has made so much steel, we're not gonna need any more for a while. So I want you to go home. I'll call you if I want you to work again.'

The steel-working men walked slowly home. No work meant no money. And that meant no food on the table or shoes on their children's feet.

They turned and looked back at the mill. No furnace firelight dancing against the window-panes. No clouds billowing black out of the smoke-stacks. Nothing but stillness and sadness and rust.

And inside the mill there was only Joe, sitting in Furnace Number Nine, a little steel tear running down his big steel cheek.

'This is my fault,' he whispered to the dirty walls. 'I ate like a donkey and worked like a donkey, and now my friends have no jobs. I must do something to help them.'

The clocks in the houses of the steel-working men ticked away hours and days and weeks and months. Their families were hungry. Their hopes were fading. And then, one night, just as the clock struck nine, they saw it, down in the valley—a furnace burning in the mill!

They rushed out of their houses and down the crooked hillside streets. They burst into the mill itself. And that's when they heard it— the very same sound they'd heard on the night that Joe came tramping through the twilight—the rumbling, tumbling sound that steel makes as it bubbles and boils in the furnace.

They followed that sound, and it led them to Furnace Number Nine. And there, in the furnace, was the head of Joe Magarac, floating on a white-hot pool of steel.

'Joe! Get out of there!' they shouted.

But Joe just laughed. 'Don't worry about me,' he said. 'I was the reason you lost your jobs. And now I'm gonna fix that. When I am all melted down, I want you to pour me out into steel beams, 'cause my steel is the strongest steel there is. Then I want you to tear down this old mill and use my beams to make a new one. A bigger one. One that will make jobs for you and your children for years to come!'

The big man said, 'Goodbye!' and then the head of Joe Magarac disappeared into the boiling steel and he was never seen again.

The men did what Joe told them, and the next year there was another strong man contest in the new steel yard. And the prize? It was the privilege of tending the fires in Furnace Number Nine—the furnace where Joe Magarac had sacrificed himself for everyone in the steel-making valley.

The Crafty Farmer

Farmer Yasohachi pasted the bright sign on the side of the village hall:

SUNDAY MORNING—COME AND SEE!

FARMER YASOHACHI CLIMBS TO HEAVEN!

People passed by and pointed. Some smiled. Many more laughed. But one person was not happy at all, for he was Yasohachi's master.

'Farmer Yasohachi!' shouted the master. 'What are you thinking of? All the other farmers have ploughed their fields. They are ready for planting. But your field lies hard and lumpy while you waste your time with silly games!'

'Oh, they are not silly, not silly at all!' grinned Farmer Yasohachi. 'Come on Sunday and see.'

Sunday morning arrived, and a great crowd gathered in one corner of Yasohachi's field. Most of the people from the village were there, including Farmer Yasohachi's master.

Farmer Yasohachi set up a tall bamboo pole in the middle of the crowd. Then he bowed and smiled and started to climb up the pole.

He clambered a quarter of the way.

He clambered a third of the way.

He clambered half the way!

And then the pole began to teeter and totter, to bend and sway, until, at last, both Yasohachi and the pole fell to the ground with a crash!

Someone moaned. Someone else booed. But Yasohachi was not flustered, not at all. He dusted himself off, picked up the pole, and marched to another corner of the field.

This time, he planted the pole much deeper. He bowed once more and, as the crowd whispered and watched and shuffled their feet, he began to climb again.

A quarter of the way.

A third of the way.

Half the way.

Two thirds of the way!

But, once again, the pole began to sway. Yasohachi tried to keep his balance, but it was no use, and he fell to the ground with a crash!

'Still not deep enough,' he muttered to the crowd. And, even though some of them were muttering by this time too, they followed him to yet another corner of his field.

Again Yasohachi planted the pole. Again Yasohachi bowed. Again Yasohachi started to

climb. But this attempt was no better, so again Yasohachi fell to the ground with a crash!

'No. Please!' he called to the crowd, as they began to walk away. 'One more chance, I beg you!'

The crowd sighed and grumbled, but, one by one, they slowly followed Yasohachi to the last corner of his field.

They huddled round and stamped their feet impatiently, and as soon as the pole again began to topple, they walked angrily away.

Yasohachi picked himself up and dusted off his dirty clothes. He was grinning from ear to ear!

'What are you smiling about, you silly man?' asked Yasohachi's master. 'You could have been ploughing your field this morning, but instead you made a fool of yourself in front of the whole village!'

'Fool?' asked Yasohachi. 'I don't think so. Take a good look at my field.'

Yasohachi's master looked, shook his head in amazement, and looked again.

Where there had once been nothing but hard, unploughed clumps of dirt there was now a field, soft and flat and ready for planting—trampled smooth by the feet of the crowd that had come to stare at Farmer Yasohachi!

Tiger Tries to Cheat

'Help me!' cried Tiger. 'Help me, somebody, please!'

Tiger was trapped. During the night, an earthquake had sent a huge boulder rolling across the front of his dark cave door. And now he couldn't get out.

'Help me! Help me, please!' he cried again.

And that's when Rabbit hopped by.

'Is that you, Tiger?' Rabbit asked.

'Of course it's me,' whined Tiger. 'Push the stone away and let me out!'

Rabbit pushed and pushed, but he could not move the heavy stone. No, not one bit. So he scurried off to find some help.

He found Elephant. And Buffalo. And Crocodile. And, along with Rabbit, they pushed and pushed and pushed, until they pushed that stone away.

Tiger leaped out of his cave. But instead of saying, 'Thank you very much!' or, 'I'm terribly grateful!', he grabbed Rabbit by the ears and shouted, 'GOTCHA!'

'Wait just a minute!' Rabbit shouted to the others. 'I helped Tiger out of his cave, and now he wants to eat me. I don't know about the rest of you, but I don't think this is fair!'

Elephant and Buffalo and Crocodile glanced at one another. Then they looked at Tiger.

'No,' they said nervously, at last. 'Not fair— not fair at all.'

'But I've got him!' complained Tiger. 'I've finally got him! After all these years!'

'Look,' said Rabbit to them all. 'Everyone knows that Tortoise is the wisest and the fairest creature in the jungle. Let's share our little problem with him.'

Elephant and Buffalo and Crocodile nodded. They liked this plan.

So Tiger sighed and nodded, too. 'All right,' he agreed. 'We'll talk to Tortoise.'

So Tortoise was sent for. But as he arrived, Tiger bent down and whispered into Tortoise's ear. 'This had better go my way,' he growled. 'It's been some time since I've had a nice bowl of tortoise soup!'

Tortoise looked at Tiger and cleared his throat. He did not like threats. No, not one bit.

'Tell me,' he said. 'What is your problem?'

Both Tiger and Rabbit began to explain at the same time, so Tortoise stopped them.

'Wait, it's confusing if you both speak at once. Why not show me?' he said. 'Show me what happened.'

'I was inside the cave,' Tiger explained.

'Then into the cave you go,' ordered Tortoise.

'And the big boulder,' explained Rabbit, 'was in front of the cave door.'

'Then let's have it back there again,' Tortoise commanded.

So Rabbit and his friends pushed the boulder back—and trapped Tiger in the cave!

'And then what happened?' asked Tortoise.

'Well, I ran to get help,' said Rabbit. 'But once we had freed Tiger he grabbed me and tried to eat me.'

'Ah,' grinned Tortoise, his wise eyes sparkling. 'So, if you had never set Tiger free, we wouldn't have a problem at all?'

'No!' Now Rabbit was grinning, too. 'No, we wouldn't.'

'Then I say we leave things as they are,' announced Tortoise, 'and solve this problem before it even starts.'

Rabbit thanked Tortoise for his wise decision. Elephant and Buffalo and Crocodile agreed.

And Tiger? For all anyone knows, he may be sitting in that cave and sulking to this very day.

The Two Brothers

Once upon a time there lived two brothers. Silverio, the oldest, was very rich. He was also greedy and deceitful. Manoel was the younger, but even though he was honest and hard-working, he was very poor.

One day, when he could not bear to look at his hungry wife and children any longer, Manoel went to visit Silverio.

'Help me, please!' he begged. 'If you were to give me the use of even a little of your land, I could grow enough to feed my family.'

Silverio thought carefully. He had the chance to do something good. But instead he decided to play an evil trick on his poor brother.

'Yes, of course,' Silverio smiled, slyly. 'On the western edge of my property there is a piece of land I have just purchased from Old Tomaso. You may grow your crops on that.'

Manoel bowed and thanked his brother. What he did not know was that the piece of land was a desert—good for nothing but growing thistles and weeds and straggly bushes.

The next day, Manoel and his wife went to look at the land.

'I can't believe your greedy brother is helping us,' said Manoel's wife. 'There must be something wrong with this land.'

'Or perhaps my brother has changed,' said Manoel, hopefully. 'We shall see.'

And so they did. They took one look at the land and knew they had been tricked!

'We will never feed our children from this land!' wept Manoel's wife.

But just as Manoel went to wipe away her tears, he saw something gleaming, shiny and bright, in the middle of a desert bush.

Manoel took his wife's hand, and together they walked toward the shiny thing. They thought it was an enormous gourd, but when they got closer, they saw that it was a wasps' nest—a huge wasps' nest—made entirely of gold.

Manoel's wife clapped her hands and hugged her husband tight.

'We're rich!' she shouted. 'We're rich! Now we can buy a good piece of land and never again have to worry about feeding our children!'

But Manoel just stood there, quietly, shaking his head.

'My darling,' he sighed. 'Silverio said we could use this land. He did not say we could keep whatever we found on it. This golden wasps' nest belongs to him.'

'Manoel! Manoel!' his wife complained. 'Sometimes you are too honest. Your brother tried to trick us, and now we have the better of him. He need never know about this treasure.'

'No,' Manoel insisted. 'He must. That is the right thing to do. The honest thing.' So he took his wife's hand and they went to see his brother.

'A golden wasps' nest?' exclaimed Silverio, when Manoel had told him the story. 'How interesting.' And his greedy mind went to work at once.

'What if there are more wasps' nests?' he wondered. 'And what if my brother or his wife is not so honest the next time? No, I think that I'd better keep this land for myself.'

'I'll tell you what,' said Silverio, at last. 'I should have given you the use of a much

99

nicer piece of land! There is a little plot to the south which is much better for growing crops.'

'Thank you,' said Manoel. 'You are so generous!' And off he went to look at the new spot, which proved to be very good indeed.

Silverio, of course, travelled west, just as fast as his horse could carry him. But when he got there, there were no golden wasps' nests to be found. His greedy, deceitful eyes could see only ordinary grey nests.

'I've been tricked!' he grumbled. 'Manoel saw that this land was a desert and made up a story so I would give him a better piece.

'Well,' he grinned evilly, 'we shall see who is the better trickster in this family!' And he carefully scooped one of the wasps' nests into his brown leather bag, and hurried off to Manoel's house.

'Manoel!' he called, when he arrived. 'I have a wonderful surprise for you! I have brought you another of those famous wasps' nests!'

'How generous!' cried Manoel to his wife. 'You see, my brother is not so bad after all!'

'Shut your windows,' Silverio ordered. 'We don't want anyone stealing such a valuable treasure. Now open the door, just a crack, and I shall push it in to you.'

Manoel did as his brother told him, and, when everything was ready, Silverio pushed the leather bag with the wasps' nest through the doorway. Then he pulled the door shut and ran off laughing.

The angry wasps darted out of the nest and buzzed around the room. But as soon as Manoel looked on them with his honest eyes, they turned to gold and fell, clinking like coins, to the ground below! Then the nest turned to gold as well. Manoel and his family were rich at last!

The next day, Manoel went to visit his brother one more time.

Silverio was amazed. His brother was not angry. His brother was not hurt. In fact, he was smiling as he bowed and said, 'Thank you for your wonderful gift.'

Then Manoel hurried off, bought a huge piece of fertile land and, to his greedy brother's even greater amazement, became the wealthiest farmer in the country!

Kayoku and the Crane

Snow fell white against the black night sky. Winter had come to the mountain where Kayoku, the woodcutter, lived with his aged mother.

'I'm cold,' the old woman whispered to her son. So he scraped together what little money he had and set off the next morning to buy her a quilt in the village below.

He was halfway there when he heard a cry, and saw a crane, slender and white, held fast to the rich black earth by a hunter's cruel snare.

Kayoku felt sorry for the beautiful bird, so he took out his knife and cut the snare—string by string—until the crane was free.

Just as the bird flew away, however, the hunter who had set the trap crept up behind Kayoku.

'What do you think you're doing?' he demanded. 'I worked hard to catch that bird and now you have set her free! You must pay me what she is worth.'

'But I only have a little money!' Kayoku explained. 'Enough to buy a quilt and no more.'

'That will do nicely,' the hunter grinned. And so Kayoku gave the man all the money he had.

There was no need to go to the village now, so Kayoku went straight home and told his mother what had happened. She was pleased that he had rescued the crane, and told him so, but she was still cold that night and longed for a soft, warm quilt.

Late the next day, someone knocked on Kayoku's door. It was already growing dark, so he opened the door carefully and there stood a girl—a beautiful girl—with skin white as rice and hair black as coal!

'I'm all alone!' the girl explained. 'And it's getting very late. Could I possibly stay in your house for the night?'

Kayoku was at a loss for words, so he looked at his mother.

101

'This is a very poor house,' she said.

'Especially for one so beautiful as you!' Kayoku added, shyly.

'But this is the only house around,' the girl pleaded. 'And it will be dark soon.'

'Yes, yes,' Kayoku said, at last. 'If you do not mind our humble little dwelling, we will be happy to welcome you.'

So the beautiful girl stayed the night. And all Kayoku could do was dream of her. Imagine his surprise, then, when she took him aside the next morning and asked if he would marry her!

'But I am just a poor woodcutter,' he said. 'And you... you are beautiful enough to be a princess!'

'But it is you I love,' she said. 'Your kind face. Your generous heart. It would make me so happy to be your wife.'

So Kayoku asked his mother and soon he and the beautiful girl were married. But even though they were very happy, the winter dragged on and on, and Kayoku's mother still had no quilt.

One bitter morning, Kayoku's wife took him aside and said very solemnly, 'I am going to make a quilt for your mother. I will go into my room. I will stay there for three days. And you must promise not to come in and disturb me.'

Kayoku thought this was strange, but he promised anyway. And three days later, his

wife came out of the room. She looked pale and thin and tired. But in her hands she held the most amazing quilt Kayoku had ever seen. It was white—white as rice—and it was made entirely of feathers!

'What a beautiful quilt!' Kayoku's mother exclaimed. 'But it is far too grand for the likes of us.'

'It is a quilt of a thousand feathers,' Kayoku's wife explained. 'And if we take it and sell it to the lord down in the village, I am sure he will give us enough money to buy plenty of ordinary quilts—and much more besides.'

So Kayoku took the quilt to the village and showed it to the lord. And not only did the lord give him two thousand gold pieces for it, he asked for another one as well.

'I... I don't know about that,' Kayoku stammered. 'It makes my wife very thin and tired.'

But the lord would not take 'no' for an answer. 'Bring me another quilt,' he said sternly. 'Or there will be trouble for you and your whole family!'

So Kayoku returned to his little house on the mountain, glad for the gold jingle-jangling in his money bag, but worried about what the lord's demands would mean for his beautiful wife.

It was just as he feared. When he told his wife that the lord wanted another quilt, he could see the weariness in her eyes.

'This one will take a week,' she sighed. 'And, once again, you must promise not to enter the room.'

Kayoku promised and, as he watched his wife shut the door, he could only think of how much he truly loved her.

He waited one day, two days, three days. He waited four days, five days, and six.

But in the middle of the seventh day, Kayoku could stand it no longer. He called his wife's name, but there was no answer. He banged on the door—there was no answer still. And so, unable to control his worry and his fear, Kayoku threw the door open, and gasped at what he saw!

For standing in front of him was not his wife at all, but a tall slender crane, plucked clean of every feather. And at the crane's feet lay another beautiful quilt.

'I am the crane you saved from the hunter's snare,' the bird explained. 'Out of gratitude for your kindness, I took the shape of a beautiful girl and vowed to be your wife forever. But now... now you have seen my true shape. And so, sadly, I must leave you.'

And with that, the window flew open and a flock of cranes filled the room. They wrapped their wings around the naked crane and carried her off into the sky until they looked no bigger than snowflakes, delicate and white, against the black mountainside.

And even though Kayoku sold the second quilt and became a wealthy man, he felt poor forevermore, for he never saw his beautiful crane-wife again.

The Two Sisters

There once lived a woman with two daughters. The oldest was rude and bad-tempered, much like the mother herself. But the youngest was kind and gentle. And for that reason, the other two women took advantage of her and forced her to do the hardest housework.

'Take this bucket!' the mother shouted at her younger daughter, one day. 'And bring us fresh water from the well!'

Unfortunately, the well was an hour's walk away. And the bucket was very heavy. But the younger daughter smiled and did as she was told.

She picked up the bucket. She walked and walked and walked. And when she came at last to the well, she filled the bucket with water and started for home.

Along the way, she met an old woman.

'I am so thirsty, my dear,' the old woman begged. 'And I have no bucket of my own. Could you, perhaps, give me a drink from yours?' The younger daughter felt sorry for the old woman.

'Of course!' she said. 'Here, let me help you.' And she lifted the heavy bucket to the old woman's lips.

What she did not know, however, was that the old woman was really a fairy in disguise!

'Thank you, my dear.' said the old woman, as she wiped her lips on her sleeve. 'Your kind words and deeds are as beautiful as flowers and precious as jewels. So from now on, whenever you speak, that is what will drop from your mouth.'

The younger daughter was puzzled. This was the most peculiar thing anyone had ever said to her. But she didn't want to hurt the old woman's feelings, so she smiled politely and carried her heavy bucket home.

'Where have you been?' her mother shouted, when the girl walked through the door. 'We're dying of thirst!'

But when the younger daughter tried to explain, rubies and roses and daffodils and diamonds came tumbling out of her mouth!

Her mother was amazed, and immediately called for the older daughter.

'Here!' she ordered, shoving the bucket at the older daughter. 'Take this bucket to the well and fill it!'

'Take it yourself!' the older daughter snapped back. 'I don't do that kind of work!'

'Well you'll do it today!' her mother hissed. 'And if an old woman asks you for a drink, you'll give it to her. And then jewels will fall from your mouth, too.'

So the older daughter trudged off to the well, grumbling and complaining all the way. She filled her bucket and started for home. But instead of an old woman, she met a beautiful princess. It was the fairy, of course, in a very different disguise!

'I'm so thirsty.' said the princess. 'I don't suppose you could give me drink?'

'Who do you think I am?' snapped the older daughter. 'One of your serving girls? If you want a drink, you can go and get it yourself!'

'I see,' said the princess. 'Your harsh words and deeds are as cruel as serpents and ugly as toads. So from now on, whenever you speak, that is what will drop from your mouth.'

'Stupid woman!' thought the older daughter. But when she returned home and tried to explain what had happened, the fairy's curse came true—toads and lizards and snakes leaped out of her open mouth!

'You've tricked us!' the mother shouted at her younger daughter. 'Look what you've done to your sister!'

'But it's not my fault, mother!' pleaded the girl, a precious jewel accompanying every word.

'Get out!' her mother shouted. 'Get out and never come back!'

So the younger daughter left. And, while the mother and the older daughter battled with snakes and toads for the rest of their lives, the younger girl met a handsome prince who asked her to marry him.

And so she ruled at his side—with words beautiful as flowers and deeds precious as jewels—and lived happily ever after.

The Selfish Beasts

One evening, Lion, Vulture, and Hyena were chewing on an antelope.

'I've been thinking,' said Lion. 'The three of us are friends. We like the same kind of food. Why don't we share a house together?'

'An excellent idea!' squawked Vulture, as he picked a bone clean.

'I couldn't agree more!' yapped Hyena. 'But I do think we should set some rules first, so that we don't upset each other.'

'Well there's only one thing that bothers me,' Lion growled. 'And that's staring. I can't stand it when someone stares at me. It's so rude!'

'Oh, I don't mind that,' squawked Vulture. 'But it does upset me if anyone makes fun of my head-feathers. They're so beautiful and full, my pride and joy!'

'What I can't stand,' said Hyena, 'is gossip! I'm not perfect. I'll admit that. My front legs are longer than my back ones. But when I find out that the other animals have been talking about me, it drives me crazy!'

So Lion, Vulture, and Hyena built a home together. And the next morning, while Lion yawned and Vulture cooked breakfast, Hyena went out for a walk.

But as soon as he stepped out of the door,

Lion said to Vulture, 'I don't know why Hyena is so sensitive about his legs. Surely it would be much worse if they were ALL short!'

What Lion didn't know was that Hyena had not walked very far. He heard what Lion said about him and came rushing back through the door. But he didn't say a thing. He just stared at Lion angrily and growled.

'What did I tell you?' Lion roared. 'I can't abide staring!'

'And I can't stand gossip!' Hyena snapped back.

And so they began to claw and bite and wrestle and fight.

Vulture tried to stay out of it, but when Lion kicked over his cooking pot and sent the hot coals flying at Vulture's head, he too became angry and joined the battle.

'Enough! Enough!' roared Lion at last. 'It is clear that we cannot live together. We must go our separate ways and never meet again.'

The other two licked their wounds and nodded in agreement. And the three of them left the little house for good.

And so, even to this day, Lion always eats alone. When he has had enough, he leaves. And then, and only then, does Hyena come to gnaw on what is left.

And Vulture? Vulture only comes floating down from the sky when Hyena is gone—to pick at the bones and sing his sad, squawking song. For when the hot coals landed on Vulture, they burnt away his beautiful head-feathers and left him bald forever!

The Determined Frog

Splish and splash. Jump and croak. Frog hopped in and out of the muddy pond.

His mother was there. His father, too. And all twenty-seven brothers and sisters—diving and swimming and paddling about.

'There must be more to life than this muddy pond,' Frog said to himself, one day.

So, splish and splash, jump and croak, he hopped away from the pond and across the farmyard.

He passed the pen where the pigs lay, and the little hut where the chickens clucked. And came, at last, to the barn.

'Now this is interesting,' he thought. And Frog hopped inside.

The barn was huge! The barn was empty! So he spent the whole day hopping—from here to hay, and hay to there. And, as the sun slipped beneath the window-sills and sent the shadows lengthening, Frog took one last, long leap—and landed, KERPLUNK, in a pitcher of cream!

Splish and splash. Jump and croak.

'Oh dear,' thought Frog. 'This is the strangest water I ever swam in. And the slipperiest, too!'

Frog tried to climb out of the pitcher, but he kept slipping back down the sides. And, because the pitcher was so deep, he could not push his feet against the bottom and jump out either.

'I'm stuck here!' Frog realized at last. And then he croaked and croaked for help. But the barn was still empty. It was dark outside, now. And his family was far away.

Splish and splash. Jump and croak.

Frog paddled and paddled, trying hard to keep his head above the cream. But he knew that, sooner or later, his strength would give out and he would slip to the bottom of the pitcher and drown.

So Frog thought and thought. He thought of his mother, and how he would miss her happy croaking in the morning.

'I can't give up and I won't give up!' Frog grunted to himself. And he paddled even harder.

Then Frog thought of his father, and how they would never again catch flies together with their long, sticky tongues.

'I can't give up and I won't give up!' Frog grunted again. And he paddled harder still.

Finally, Frog thought of his brothers and sisters, and how he would miss playing hop-tag and web-tackle with them.

'I CAN'T GIVE UP AND I WON'T GIVE UP!' Frog grunted and shouted and groaned. Then he paddled as hard as he could.

And that's when Frog's feet felt something. The cream under his webbed toes was no longer wet and slippery. Instead, it was hard and lumpy. For with all his paddling, Frog had churned that cream into butter!

Frog rested his feet against the butter. He pushed hard with his strong back legs. And with a grunt and a shove, he leaped out of the pitcher and onto the barn floor.

Then the frog who would not give up hopped straight back home, and lived happily ever after, splishing and splashing, jumping and croaking, with his family in the muddy pond.

The Robber and the Monk

Once there was a monk. A little monk who lived by himself in a little clay hut. He prayed. He wove baskets from palm leaves. And when people from the city came to visit, he tried to help them with their problems.

The little monk wore a coarse brown robe, ate bread and broth, and had almost nothing to call his own. Except for a book—a very special book—which he treasured and read every day.

One day, a robber came to visit the monk. A big robber. A bad robber. With a great, bushy beard and a long, sharp sword.

'Give me your treasure!' he shouted.

So the little monk gave him the book—the very special book—and watched sadly as the robber rode away.

When the robber reached the city, he went to see a shopkeeper.

'I have no use for books!' he complained. 'I need gold—and lots of it! Tell me what this book is worth, and I shall sell it.'

'I cannot say,' said the shopkeeper, flicking through the pages. 'But I know someone who can. Leave it with me for a day or two, and I will ask him.'

'All right!' growled the robber, pulling out his sword. 'I will return in two days. Make sure the book is here when I get back!'

Later that day, when the shop had closed, the shopkeeper climbed on his donkey and rode out into the desert. He rode for mile after dusty mile until he came at last to a little clay hut. And he went in to visit the little monk!

'I have a book,' he explained. 'A big man with a bushy beard brought it to me. He wants to sell it. Can you tell me how much it is worth?' Then he pulled the book out of his bag and showed it to the monk.

The little monk stared at the book. He had never imagined that he would see his treasure again. But he did not grab for it and shout, 'This is mine!' or point his finger at the shopkeeper and say, 'Your customer is a thief!'

No, all he said was, 'This is a very valuable book, worth a year's wages, at least.' Then he bid the shopkeeper farewell.

When the robber returned to the city, he was in a terrible mood.

'So tell me,' he grunted. 'How much is my book worth?'

'A great deal!' grinned the shopkeeper. 'A year's wages, at least!'

The robber's mood changed at once.

'Excellent!' he smiled. 'And... how can you be sure of that?'

'That's easy,' explained the shopkeeper. 'There is a little monk who lives out in the desert, in a little clay hut. He knows all about these things. I took the book and I showed it to him!'

The robber's mood changed once again.

'A little monk?' he stammered. 'Out in the desert?'

'That's right.'

'And you told him I wanted to sell the book?'

'A big man with a bushy beard—that's what I said.'

'And he said nothing more about the book? Nothing about me?'

'No, of course not. Why should he?' asked the shopkeeper.

'No reason,' lied the robber. 'No reason at all.'

Then he grabbed the book, and dashed out of the shop—as quick as a thief!

He rode out into the desert, mile after dusty mile, until he came to the little clay hut.

'What is this all about?' he shouted, as he burst through the door. 'You could have turned me in and had me arrested. But instead you said nothing!'

'That's right,' the monk nodded. 'For I had already forgiven you.'

'Forgiven me?' the robber cried. 'Forgiven *me?*' And then his voice grew very quiet. No one has ever forgiven me!' he whispered. 'Hated me, chased me, vowed to take revenge—yes. But forgiven? Never!'

And at that moment, something melted in the heart of the big, bad robber. He pulled the book out of his sack and gave it to the little monk.

'This is yours,' he said meekly. 'I can keep it no longer.'

The monk smiled, and thanked the robber. He invited him to stay in the little hut—to learn more about forgiveness and peace. And it wasn't long before that robber became a monk himself—a big, bushy-bearded monk who shared with others what little he had and lived happily ever after!

A Note from the Author

With the exception of 'The Generous Bird', all the stories in this book are retellings of traditional tales from around the world. They have been retold by many people over the years and I am just the next in a long line of storytellers. Each of us uses slightly different words and phrases, and so the stories evolve. You may wish to read other versions of some of these stories, so I would like to acknowledge some of the sources I have referred to, although most of these stories can be found in several collections.

'Three Months' Night' from 'One Night, One Day' in *Tales of the Nimipoo* by E.B. Heady, World Publishing Co, New York. 'Arion and the Dolphin' from 'The Boy and the Dolphin' in *Old Greek Fairy Tales* by R. Lancelyn Green, G. Bell & Sons Ltd, London. The 'Rabbit and Tiger' stories from *The Tiger and the Rabbit and Other Tales* by P. Belpre, J.B. Lippincott & Co. 'The Shepherd and the Clever Princess' from 'Timo and the Princess Vendla' and 'The Amazing Pine Cone' from 'The Two Pine Cones' in *Tales from a Finnish Tupa* by J. Lloyd Bowman and M. Blanco, A. Whitman & Co, Chicago. 'Tortoise Brings Food' from 'Uwungelema' and 'The Very Strong Sparrow' from 'The Strongest Sparrow in the Forest' in *African Fairy Tales* by K. Arnott, Frederick Muller Ltd, London. 'The Mouse Deer's Wisdom' from 'King Solomon, the Merchant and the Mouse Deer' in *Java Jungle Tales* by H. DeLeeuw, Arco Publishing, New York. 'The Four Friends' from 'The Goat, the Raven, the Rat, and the Tortoise' in *Animal Folk Tales* by B. Kerr Wilson, Hamlyn Publishing Group, London. 'The Brave Bull Calf' from 'A Little Bull Calf' in *The Gypsy Fiddle* by J. Hampden, World Publishing Co, New York. 'The Clever Mouse' from 'St Cadog and the Mouse' in *Welsh Legendary Tales* by E. Sheppard-Jones, Nelson, Edinburgh. 'The Selfish Sand Frog' from 'The Thirsty Sand Frog' and 'How the Kangaroo Got Its Tale' in *Djugurba: Tales from the Spirit Time*, Australian National University Press, Canberra. 'The Mouse's Bride' from *Fairy Tales of India* by L. Turnbull, Criterion Books, New York. 'The Big Wave' from 'Gleanings in Buddha Fields' by Lafcadio Hearn, Houghton Mifflin Co, Boston. 'The Knee-High Man' from 'The Knee-High Man' in *The Stars Fell on Alabama* by C. Carmer, Farrar and Rinehart, New York. 'The Clever Baker' from 'The Woman Who Flummoxed the Fairies' in *Heather and Broom* by S.N. Leodhas, Holt, Rinehart and Winston, New York. 'The Greedy Farmer' from 'The Marvellous Cow of Clyn Barfog' in *Elves and Ellefolk* by N.M. Belting, Holt, Rinehart, and Winston, New York. 'Lazy Tom' from 'The Field of Boliauns' in *Fairy Tales from the British Isles* by A. Williams-Ellis, Frederick Warne & Co, London. 'The Contented Priest' from 'The Gardener, the Abbot and the King' in *Bungling Pedro and Other Majorcan Tales* by A. Mehdevi, Alfred A. Knopf, New York. 'Olle and the Troll' from 'The Old Troll of the Big Mountain' in *The Faber Book of Northern Folktales* by K. Crossley-Holland, Faber & Faber, London. 'The Steel Man' from *Joe Magarac and His USA Citizen Papers* by I. Shapiro, University of Pittsburgh Press, Pittsburgh. 'The Crafty Farmer' from 'Crafty Yasohachi Climbs to Heaven' and 'Kayoku and the Crane' from 'The Cloth of a Thousand Feathers' in *Men from the Village Deep in the Mountains*, translated by G. Bang, Collier Macmillan Publishers, London. 'The Two Brothers' from 'The Golden Gourd' in *South American Wonder Tales* by F. Carpenter, Follett Publishing Company, New York. 'The Selfish Beasts' from 'Why the Lion, the Vulture, and the Hyena Do Not Live Together' in *Olode the Hunter and Other Tales from Nigeria* by H. Courlander, Harcourt, Brace & World Inc, New York. 'The Determined Frog' from 'The Wise Frog and the Foolish Frog' in *Tales from Central Russia* by J. Riordan, Kestrel Books, London. 'The Robber and the Monk' from *The Desert Fathers*, translated by H. Waddell, Collins Publishers, London.